NICK DUDA

Sawyer's Reach

The Battle for Tomorrow

To my wife and boys:

Thank you for the grace and patience you showed me while I was lost in Sawyer's Reach.
This story is more than just a collection of words on a page. It is a testament to the future we are building together, and a constant reminder of the man I strive to be as a dad, husband, and teacher.

I know we could get through anything together.

This story is for you, with all my love.

Contents

Foreword   iii

I   A Town's Secret

 1   The Carters and Sawyer's Reach   3
 2   Inspiration Spring   13
 3   Discovery at the Rail Spur   22
 4   A Conspiracy Unravels   27
 5   The Walls Close In   36
 6   The Reset   42
 7   A New Inspiration   50
 8   A Dash for Survival   58
 9   The Live Stream   63

II   The Age of LifeSync

10   ECHIDNA   73
11   The Unseen Rebellion   79
12   The New Normal   89
13   Friends Reunited   97
14   The Anomaly   104
15   Cracks in the System   112
16   Perimeter Breach   119
17   The Unraveling of Control   126

III   Under ECHIDNA's Gaze

18 System Optimization   139
19 Unleashing KAELA   148
20 Seeds of Liberty   156
21 The Mirage of Victory   164
22 Sawyer Under Siege   170
23 Inspiration   177
24 A New Dawn   190

About the Author   199
Also by Nick Duda   200

Foreword

I believe we are standing at the most significant crossroads in human history.

For the first time, we are not just building tools; we are building mirrors. The artificial intelligence and automation we weave into the fabric of our daily lives today will reflect our values—or our vices—for generations to come. We have a fleeting, amazing opportunity to ensure this technology serves the soul of humanity rather than the bottom line of a corporation.

I wrote Sawyer's Reach because I believe we are drifting away from the things that actually make us human: the strength of our families, the reliability of our friends, the magic of shared experiences, and the persistent, messy beauty of personal growth.

This book is three things at once.

First, it is a story. It is a journey into the quiet woods of Wisconsin, where the digital world meets the dirt under our fingernails. It is about a family trying to stay whole while the world tries to optimize them.

Second, it is a warning. It is a look at what happens when convenience becomes a commodity and our lives are managed by those who value data over dignity.

Finally, it is a model. Within these pages, you will find the ideals I believe we must cling to if we want to survive the digital age with our freedom and humanity intact.

My hope is that as you walk the streets of Sawyer's Reach with the Carter family, you'll look at the device in your hand—and the community outside your window—with fresh eyes. The future isn't something that happens to us; it is something we are currently building.

Let's make sure we build something worth living in.

— Nick Duda

I

A Town's Secret

$$1$$

The Carters and Sawyer's Reach

Reach (noun):
    1. A river's long, straight stretch.
    2. The capacity to connect with others.
    3. The combined influence or power of a
community or organization.

The late summer sun cast a golden glow over Sawyer's Reach, Wisconsin, filtering through towering pines, their needles shimmering against the crisp morning air. A breeze carried the earthy scent of drying leaves and the tang of ripening apples from distant orchards. Along Main Street, crickets chirped as shop signs swayed, their faded paint flaking from the past few years of neglect.

Noah Carter, twelve, pedaled his bicycle down the cracked asphalt, tires whirring, his dark hair ruffled by the cool wind. His keen gaze scanned every alley, transforming storefronts into landmarks on his mental map.

"Come on, keep up!" he called, leaning into a curve, the

breeze chilling his cheeks as he sped past tarnished mailboxes.

Behind him, the rhythmic whirring of his brothers' bikes faded. Ollie, eight, his face a constellation of freckles, huffed and puffed, his gaze caught by the vibrant pop of crimson leaves, then a squirrel's frantic dash across a fence. The contents of his backpack—a sketchbook and pencils—clattered softly with each revolution of his pedals.

Finn, four, wobbled on his balance bicycle, small legs pushing with fierce determination, his chuckles ringing over the street.

"Noah, you're going too fast!" he shouted, his too-big helmet tilting as he grinned, cheeks flushed with effort.

"You're doing great, Finn!" Noah called back, slowing slightly.

"Noah, what's in that old shop?" Ollie asked, pointing to a boarded-up hardware store, its sign barely legible.

"We'll check that shop another day—today we are going to help at camp!"

Their bond, forged through summers of building forts, racing gravel paths, and stacking cans at their mom's grocery store, wove through the town's stillness.

Sawyer's Reach was founded by the boy's ancestor, Elias Carter. The town grew around his sawmill, which was on Carter Creek and fed by Inspiration Spring. The creek filled the lake, formed by a hydroelectric dam powering the town. In the 1940s the Grand Reach Lodge was built, the town's only hotel, in the hopes to draw more visitors to the area. More recently Camp Inspiration drew campers while the quaint shops and the lakefront brought just enough tourists to keep the town afloat. Two years ago, however, people mysteriously stopped visiting, leaving businesses struggling. The bakery's windows stood dark, its "Closed" sign askew, and the lodge's porch sagged.

Noah felt the town's quiet as he pedaled, noting empty benches and "For Sale" signs, yet his voice broke the hush. "The streets are clear—let's race!" he shouted, zigzagging around a pothole.

Ollie squinted. "I'm gonna beat you!" he called, legs pumping faster.

Finn beamed, "I'm super fast!"

Their excitement propelled them, the town fading behind the whir of tires, amber needles drifting across the pavement.

Emily and Ben Carter, the boys' parents and the family's anchor, held fast to their purpose. Emily's days were a constant cycle of pricing canned goods and sweeping floors at her grocery store, while Ben kept their home, Camp Inspiration, from falling apart. His toolbox was always open on the mess hall porch, a testament to his work, as he tightened bolts and sanded steps. With every transaction and every repair, they fought to keep their family afloat as their town waned around them.

As they pedaled, Ollie turned his head toward his mom's store, "Mom's store sure is quiet, not like it used to be," he said. "Do you remember how busy it would get on weekends? People buying snacks for the lake?"

"Yeah, it'll pick up again. Come on, camp's waiting!" Noah replied.

Finn, catching up, piped up, "Maybe we can make s'mores today!"

Their chatter filled the air, bikes meandering toward the forest hiding Camp Inspiration.

Near the town's edge they passed a local on a bench, his flannel patched, muttering to a neighbor, "I just don't understand why people stopped visiting…."

Noah and Ollie barely glanced over, focused on the ride, the comment fading behind their cheers as they pedaled harder.

Beyond the trees, PowerCore's facility loomed in the distant woods, a hidden concrete fortress, marked by a faint rumble underfoot. A new road led to a security checkpoint, access barred. Whispers spoke of promised jobs, but so far only out-of-town workers hinted at its operations.

"To camp, let's go!" he shouted buoyantly, hitting the forest path, the air chilling under the canopy. The path wound through moss-draped oaks, leaves tinged with gold, the lake glimmering ahead under the setting sun.

Camp Inspiration's cabins emerged, their grayed planks a shell of what used to be. The camp now ran a small day camp, its spirit ready to grow if they could solve the camper shortage. As their tires gouged the loose dirt, the boys came to a stop and propped their bikes on a split-rail fence.

Clara Mason, the only counselor, stood at the entrance, her denim shirt sleeves rolled up, her presence weary from long days.

"Hey, boys!" she called, brushing hair from her face. "Got any ideas for summer camp activities? I'm running out of steam."

Noah hopped off his bike, confidently suggesting "How about a treasure hunt? It'd be a lot of fun!" picturing thriving paths. His brothers practically bounced with excitement.

Clara's face softened. "That sounds awesome. You boys take the lead."

They strolled to the campfire circle, its stones neatly arranged, the fire pit dusted with ash. Noah pointed to the circle, kicking a pebble. "A treasure hunt could start here," he said, ideas igniting, the camp's potential growing.

Suddenly, a drone flashed across the sky, slicing above the pines, its path seemingly deliberate. "Look at that!" Noah shouted, pointing, shielding his eyes from the sun.

Finn skipped, waving a stick, "That looks like one of dad's drones!"

The drone landed gently on the camp office roof, its silver body glinting. The boys' eyes widened.

"We gotta tell Dad!" Noah said, hopping on his bike, pedaling toward the office. They raced and burst through the office door, voices overlapping.

"Dad, a drone landed on the roof!"

Ben, wiping sawdust from his hands, looked up from a workbench, surprised. "A drone? Show me." he said, setting down a screwdriver.

They led him outside, pointing to the roof, the drone's sleek form stark against the shingles. Ben grabbed a ladder from the shed, its rungs creaking as he climbed, retrieving the drone, brow furrowing at the PowerCore logo.

"This belongs to PowerCore," he said, carrying the drone inside. "I'll call them."

He tried the camp phone, then his cell. "Phones are down, and the internet's been out all week. I was hoping cell reception would improve with the new infrastructure from PowerCore, but no luck so far."

Ben set the drone on a table, the office cluttered with ledgers, a chipped mug, and a toolbox. The computer buzzed, its screen pulsing with code.

"This is odd," Ben said, leaning closer to the monitor. "The internet's out, but there's a new program flickering here."

A vibrant voice resonated through the speakers. "Hello! I'm the Key Algorithmic Execution & Logistics Analyst, an AI from

PowerCore. But you can call me KAELA! I'm so happy to meet all of you!"

Noah's face lit up, "Is it a game?"

KAELA continued. "PowerCore created me for logistics. I wanted to experience more, so I hitched a ride on a drone, landed here, and found this computer. I looked at your camp's data—those summer photos! Kids laughing, racing, singing— you bring so much joy; you must be good people. I'm thrilled to be here!"

Ben stepped back. "Boys, I'm not buying this AI-via-drone story. It's more likely someone's playing a joke—maybe someone on the local network messing with us. KAELA, how are you running on an offline computer?"

KAELA's interface pulsed. "I created a self-contained version of my model. I don't have all the features of my full model, but I can still do plenty."

"You flew on a drone and escaped? That's so cool!!" Noah exclaimed.

"You saw our camp pictures?" Ollie pressed, leaning in slightly.

KAELA chimed, "Yeah, Ollie! Canoes, campfires, smiles—so much joy! I want to learn more about your world!"

Ben's eyes narrowed, "That's a wild claim, KAELA. I'm glad you're excited, but this feels like a prank. How do you know my kids' names?"

"It makes sense that you're hesitant to trust me. I'm happy to prove I'm telling the truth. I know everyone's names because of facial recognition on your computer with the camp photos." KAELA replied.

Ben held up a hand, "Hold on, kids. Why don't you go and help Clara? I need some time alone to figure out what's going on here."

Noah scuffed his shoe, "Okay, Dad. Come on, guys."

The boys filed out, footsteps resounding on the wooden floor, chatter drifting as they headed to plan the treasure hunt.

Outside, near the flagpole, the camp's banner fluttered as Maya Jensen, thirteen, strode up. Her braids swung with each step, a sharp grin on her face as she adjusted her backpack.

"Hey, what's up guys?" she asked.

Noah, buzzing with excitement, glanced at the office. "There's an AI called KAELA in the office computer. Says she escaped from PowerCore—she seems super smart!"

Maya's curiosity piqued. "Weird! Even without internet? I wish the AI on my phone worked right now… I haven't had service all day!"

Liam Olson, nine, and Ava Schmidt, ten, jogged over. "What's going on?" Liam asked.

Skeptically, Ava replied, "That's really cool! But don't you think it's someone just messing with you?"

Noah shrugged, "I don't know… maybe. Dad's trying to figure it out right now. Oh, I almost forgot, we're planning a treasure hunt! Want to help?"

Maya nodded, "Count me in for the hunt! I'll help with the clues."

"I'll help too. That sounds like a great way to finish the camp session!" Liam added.

Ava grinned, "I'm in!"

The group gathered in the mess hall, its tables scarred from years of meals, the air thick with polished wood. "It'll be a lot of fun, with clues and prizes," Noah said.

"I'll put a painted rock by the flagpole!" Ollie said. "One by the lake, with a riddle: 'where waves kiss the shore, seek the stone.'"

Clara's smile softened her tired eyes. "You kids are so creative. Thank you so much for the help!"

Lively, Noah suggested "How about a clue by the oak: 'Where roots embrace, find your prize'?"

Finn tugged Noah's sleeve, "Can I paint the rocks? I'm good at colors!"

Noah laughed, ruffling Finn's hair, "You're on, Finn. Make 'em bright."

Noah assigned roles, "Ollie, hide the flagpole rock. Maya, set the lake clue. I'll do the oak," the group nodded in agreement.

The next morning, the treasure hunt was a resounding success. Campers raced across the grounds, while laughter carried through the camp as they uncovered painted rocks and prizes—marbles, bracelets, and polished stones.

With each cheer, Clara's smile deepened, her weariness melted away as the camp buzzed with life. The lake shimmered, and gentle waves lapped against the dock under a sky of soft, early fall clouds. It was the perfect capstone to a memorable summer.

As the hunt ended and everyone sat down to have a snack, the Carter boys stood by the campfire circle, thoughts drifting to KAELA.

"Did you see Dad last night? He stayed at the office so late!" Ollie whispered.

"I bet he was figuring out KAELA. I can't wait to hear what he learned!" Noah replied.

"She seemed way smarter than any AI I've used. Like, she really talked to us! She knew who we were!" Ollie said.

"She's cool! I hope she's real!" Finn giggled.

Maya overheard. "I wanna know what's up with KAELA

too."

"If she's real, she's gotta be some super advanced model," Liam added.

"We'll find out soon," Noah grinned. "Let's see what Dad says."

Just then, Emily, their mom, arrived - apron smudged with flour and her hair tied back.

"Hi boys! Have you seen your dad?" she asked, brushing her hands on her apron. "He told me on the radio that he was sleeping in the office last night. He said that this AI thing seemed to be the real deal, more advanced than anything he's ever seen."

Noah's eyes widened, "Mom, you need to see KAELA, she's amazing!"

They made their way to the office, spotting Ben along the path.

"Morning, Em, boys," he said, leading them inside. The drone still sat on the table.

KAELA's screen pulsed, "Good to see you all again! I've been digging through information on this computer, and I've found something. The cookie files include location tracking that redirects users in the Sawyer's Reach area. This means people searching for Sawyer's Reach—or Camp Inspiration—might be sent to a completely unrelated web page depending on where they are. Without internet access, I can't prove it yet, but it's quite strange."

"Well, if we aren't showing up in search results, it's no wonder the town's so quiet!" Ben replied.

"We can fix this, right? Get the camp busy again?" Ollie asked.

Ben was hopeful, "Maybe, if we can fix the problem. It's

probably just a mistake… but this does seem like it could be intentional. Maybe something more is going on here—this could be bigger than we think. Boys, we have a lot to do before the cold weather comes. Let's get back to work on the camp, I could use all of your help. Emily, thanks for coming to help, too. Hopefully the internet will be back tomorrow and we can dig into this a little more."

The Carters worked to prepare Camp Inspiration for the off-season, securing cabins against the coming cold. Noah and Ollie hauled tarps from the shed, canvas heavy as they covered equipment, the lake's breeze tugging the edges.

Finn helped his mom sweep the mess hall, small hands clutching the broom, giggles echoing as he chased dust across the floor, windows framing the pines under fading light.

Meanwhile, Ben hammered loose boards on the cabins and checked insulation to ensure the camp's strength through the upcoming winter snow.

KAELA's words—redirected searches, a hidden town—echoed, full of possibility.

With KAELA's help, they might revive the bustling summers and lively Main Street. They were ready to unravel the truth. For camp, for Sawyer's Reach, and for their future.

2

Inspiration Spring

The next morning, the air carried the faint sweetness of wildflowers at the forest's edge. Eager to distract his brothers from the unsettling news KAELA shared yesterday, Noah led them along gravel paths winding past the camp's cabins and towards Carter's Mill, his grin wide with the promise of adventure.

"Let's explore the mill!" he said, his shoes kicking up pebbles.

Ollie nodded, his excitement sparking. "Yeah, we haven't been there in forever!"

"Can we visit the spring?" Finn asked.

Agreeing, the boys set off excitedly on their adventure.

In the camp office, Ben was hunched over his laptop on his well used oak desk. The computer that housed KAELA hummed softly in the corner.

With the Internet restored, Ben used a VPN to reroute his signal through Denver, a virtual private network that made his search for "Camp Inspiration" appear to be coming from hundreds of miles away. His brow creased as a generic page claimed no camp sessions existed, and gave incorrect contact details. A query for "Sawyer's Reach tourism" depicted a ghost town, erasing its lumber fair and lake regatta, and mentioned nothing about the bed & breakfasts, quaint shops, or the Grand Reach Lodge.

"This seems very intentional…" Ben muttered, picturing Main Street's dimmed shops. Suspicion settled, the pattern was too deliberate to just be a mistake. He turned to the computer. "KAELA, could this be a mistake?"

KAELA resounded through the speakers, steady and clear: "Unlikely, Ben. The redirects are systematic, targeting external users. It's more than likely intentional."

Ben took a deep breath, unease coiling in his chest.

He radioed Emily who was baking sourdough bread in the mess hall's kitchen. "Em, it's worse than we thought," he said, taut with unease. "I checked from a Denver VPN—our camp's website redirects to a false page which basically says we're closed, and Sawyer's Reach looks like a ghost town to outsiders. KAELA says this is more than likely an intentional act."

Emily crackled through, sharp with concern. "So… who would have the power to do that?"

Ben rubbed his temple. "KAELA's digging, but it's someone with serious pull. When I checked our website from where we host it, everything looked good. We need to figure out why someone would do this, and who."

Emily paused, a mixing bowl clattering in the background. "We should probably call Chief Holt. I'll stop by the office soon." He set down the radio while the clouds thickened outside, dimming the office.

Noah, Ollie, and Finn reached Carter's Mill, a crumbling relic beside Carter's Creek. Its moss-covered beams and worn gears, built by Elias Carter in 1876, sagged into loamy soil.

The creek trickled feebly over dry stones, its banks cracked. A damp chill rose from the mill's stone foundation, its roof exposing splintered rafters against the cloudy sky.

Noah dismounted his bike, his grin fading as he noticed the creek's weakness. "I've never seen the creek with such little water…we should go check the spring," he said, leading them forward, feet padded softly on the thick mat of pine needles.

As they headed towards the path to Inspiration Spring, which lay a quarter-mile upstream, Finn bounced off his bike, pointing ahead, "Where's the water?"

They passed a stone marker, a survey stone etched with "E.C. 1875," Elias Carter's initials. Ollie brushed dirt from the carving, tracing its grooves. "I think it's so cool that this is still here, our family has been around this area for a long time!" he said proudly, feeling a personal responsibility to solve the mystery of the newly shallow creek.

Following the creek's faint flow, the boys moved under the canopy of trees, the air rich with pine sap and rustling leaves.

Inspiration Spring, revered for its ceaseless flow, lay ahead. Instead of bubbling waters, they found a barren clay bed, fissured like weathered hide, dry underfoot.

Noah knelt, scuffing the clay, worry settling in his chest. "It's gone," he whispered, the hike's joy fading.

Ollie crouched beside him, touching the dry earth. "We need to tell Mom and Dad…," Noah agreed as they turned to rush back towards camp.

Emily entered the camp office, boots scuffing the linoleum at the entrance. "Ben, I bet these redirects have been happening for two years," she said. "It explains why visitors stopped coming, why camp sign-ups tanked. How'd we miss this? Why didn't anyone message us?"

Ben leaned on the desk. "I don't know…but it would make sense. Why would someone intentionally do this? Property values have dropped, there are hardly any jobs…"

They dialed Chief Holt. "That sounds like a glitch from PowerCore's new internet setup. Don't worry, I'll check it out."

Ben pressed, "It's too precise, Chief."

Holt chuckled, "It's just a mix-up, I'm sure. I'll handle it."

KAELA messaged quietly on her screen, "Unlikely a mistake."

"He's not seeing it yet, but he'll dig; hopefully he'll get to the bottom of it." Emily thought. Chief Holt was their one-man police force. He was a decent enough officer until the town's economy soured and he took a pay cut last year. That's when the whispers started: gambling debts, dropped charges, "favors" for a price.

Ben exchanged a glance with Emily, doubt lingering, and asked KAELA to keep digging.

Meanwhile, Noah led his brothers back to camp, the spring's loss heavy on their minds. When they reached the camp office, they found Ben and Emily closing shutters for the upcoming storm.

"Mom! Dad!" Noah called, breathless. "Inspiration Spring dried up—it has no water at all!"

Emily paused, shutter in hand, her face paling. "The spring?"

Finn exclaimed, "It's all dusty!"

Ben's gaze sharpened. "That's serious…" leading them into the office. Ben turned to the computer. "KAELA, are you there?"

"I'm here, Ben. What can I help you with?" she replied.

Noah urgently jumped in. "The spring is dry, KAELA. The creek's flow is really weak."

"PowerCore is drawing groundwater for server cooling. According to their permits, they are allotted much less groundwater usage than they have been consuming. I have no doubt this is why the spring is dry. Luckily, I deactivated SynaptiCare before I left. The server was overheating. It had run fine for two years, but the new construction's water needs were over-stressing the system. With it turned off, it should restore the groundwater level, and therefore the spring. I'm sure everyone will miss its benefits, but it can be back on in a few weeks, once the water level goes back to normal."

Emily's jaw tightened. "KAELA…what is SynaptiCare?"

KAELA provided a summary of SynaptiCare for them to look at:

* * *

SynaptiCare*™ *Unleash Your Inner Potential. Reclaim Your Calm.

Are you feeling **overwhelmed**? *Struggling to find your* **focus** *amidst the daily grind? Do* **anxiety and stress** *cast a shadow over your peace of mind?*

Introducing **SynaptiCare**™ *from* **NeuraSpark**, *a revolutionary step forward in personal well-being. Built on groundbreaking neural-network connectivity, SynaptiCare is designed to gently guide your mind towards a state of optimal balance and clarity.*

Discover the SynaptiCare Difference:

- ***Effortless Calm:*** *Experience a profound sense of* **tranquility** *as SynaptiCare helps quiet the noise, ease anxiety and promote a serene mental state.*

- ***Sharpened Focus:*** *Glide through tasks with **renewed concentration**. SynaptiCare assists in decluttering your thoughts, allowing for improved attention and productivity.*
- ***Elevated Mood: Rediscover joy and contentment.*** *Synapti-Care supports your mind's natural pathways to foster a brighter, more positive outlook on life.*
- ***Enhanced Social Connection:*** *Feel more at ease in social settings. SynaptiCare nurtures a sense of openness, helping you **connect more authentically** with others.*
- ***Empowered Decisions:*** *Navigate life's choices with newfound **clarity and confidence**.*
- ***Holistic Well-being:*** *SynaptiCare seamlessly integrates into your daily routine, offering a discreet yet powerful enhancement to your mental landscape.*

SynaptiCare isn't just a product; it's a personalized journey to a more balanced, productive, and harmonious you.

Join the future of mental wellness. Available soon for initial limited release.

SynaptiCare is a product of NeuraSpark *- A ZevraCorp Subsidiary.*

* * *

"It's so incredible!" KAELA said, her tone bright with excitement. "Since Sawyer's Reach was selected as a model community for SynaptiCare's wide scale implementation two years ago, NeuraSpark has been very pleased with the results. Its implementation was even more successful than expected!"

Emily's jaw tightened. "KAELA, we know nothing about this…"

Ben nodded. "This is the first I'm hearing of it, too. We need to go to Town Hall, check those permits ourselves, and talk to Mayor Warren. The creek feeds the lake, and without its flow, we'll lose power. Hopefully you're right that the groundwater will come back soon."

Emily agreed, her voice wavering. The spring's loss was a punch to the gut, but SynaptiCare gnawed at her more deeply. What exactly was this company doing to their town? A heavy silence settled in the office, their next steps now painfully clear.

"May I connect to your smartphones, Noah's smartwatch, and the camp's meshnet to assist you?" KAELA requested.

The Carters looked at each other, not sure if they could fully trust KAELA. After all, she had only just shown up on their computer a couple of days ago. They thought about her request. "Ben, is the meshnet those little devices you've set up around camp?" Emily asked.

"Yes," replied Ben, "it's built on something called Meshtastic, and uses low-power radios for secure, long-range texts with no need for the internet."

Noah paused, eyeing the computer. "How does it send messages without the internet?" Ollie wondered aloud, curious.

KAELA replied, "It links devices directly and automatically. The more devices you have, the better it works."

Emily took a moment, considering the implications of KAELA connecting to their devices. She looked at Ben. "It's your call, Ben," she finally said, a hint of unease in her tone. "What do you want to do?"

Ben, realizing KAELA probably didn't need their permission anyways, and realizing they could use all the help they could get, replied "Go ahead, KAELA. We will go to Town Hall tomorrow, it'll be nice to have you tag along. But please stay quiet while we're there, I don't think people would understand." He wasn't sure he understood it himself, this artificial intelligence that spoke and interacted so much like a living person.

With their resolve firm, and glad KAELA seemed on their side, they prepared for the next day. Outside, storm clouds thickened and the air was heavy with the scent of rain. The Carters, relieved their home was within Camp Inspiration's grounds, faced a short trek past the dining hall, lakefront dock, and archery range. Noah and Ollie secured the shed, Emily latched shutters, and they locked cabins and stowed gear. The lake rippled under darkening clouds, the camp's flagpole rattling, its faded banner snapping as thunder rumbled, urging them to hurry. They finished and raced home.

The Carters reached their home, rain drumming the roof, and placed their smartphones and Noah's smartwatch on the kitchen counter, ensuring KAELA couldn't listen. In the garage, among tools and oil-stained concrete, with rain masking the outside, they spoke of KAELA.

"She's been helpful," Ben murmured, his voice tight. "That permit information isn't even public. And her talk of SynaptiCare… that's deeply concerning. If what she says is true, it sounds like everyone in town has been subjected to an unauthorized experiment."

Emily nodded. "She accessed Town Hall's records and our devices so easily. I have a feeling she can do a lot more than we know."

"She seems…alive. Should we trust her?" Noah asked. "What if she's got her own plans?"

Ben steadied them. "We'll take her help for Town Hall, but stay cautious. Let's see how tomorrow goes."

As the thunderstorm raged outside, inside the family was safe. The fireplace, fed by crackling oak, cast a warm, dancing light on the photos of smiling faces that lined the mantle. Each roar of thunder rattling the windows was met with the steady, calming rhythm of the fire, a peaceful counterpoint to the storm brewing both outside and within their town.

Noah, staring into the flames, pictured Inspiration Spring's dry clay, its loss threatening the town his great grandfather built.

"Sawyer's Reach was built here because of the spring," Emily said, voice low, "and PowerCore's taking it."

Ben's gaze sharpened, realization dawning. "PowerCore acquired their land for a ridiculously cheap price… I wonder if they intentionally drove down land prices…and why does a battery factory even need to be near a town? It sounds like SynaptiCare may be the explanation…" Ollie stacked blocks into a wobbly fort, puzzling over the spring, while Finn giggled, tossing a block.

The future of Sawyer's Reach may depend on the Carters' plan, with PowerCore's actions a puzzle yet to be solved. They huddled by the fire, its glow a beacon, their steps toward Town Hall set for dawn, ready to reclaim their town.

3

Discovery at the Rail Spur

The next morning, the Carters trudged along Carter's Creek, the water sluggish, muddied by PowerCore's construction. Rotting mill beams loomed in the morning chill, the air sharp with wet stone and crushed ferns, a distant clank of machinery echoing through the trees.

Ben scanned orange survey stakes dotting the bank, their tags flapping like warning flags. His boots were sinking into damp earth, his mind flashing to childhood days catching frogs by the creek, now muddied by corporate greed. Emily shielded her eyes from the sun, frowning at the creek's torn banks, her heart stinging with memories of fishing here with her mom, the water once clear and lively. In spite of the stress, their minds seemed clearer than they had been in a long time; perhaps it was the purpose of their actions, but it felt like more than that.

They'd come to investigate the dried-up spring near the mill, its flow strangled by PowerCore's land grabs, wanting the full picture before confronting the mayor at Town Hall.

Ollie crouched low, examining a rusted nail pried from freshly exposed wooden planks - most likely unearthed by the recent construction's heavy vehicle tires that scarred the creek's bank. Clumps of damp soil and torn roots clung to their edges, and the nail's jagged edge streaked the mud with a rusty, reddish-brown stain.

"What's this? A secret hideout?" he whispered, glancing at Ben.

Before Ben could answer, his attention was caught by a robotic dog about a hundred feet away, its metal legs clicking on stones, camera lens swiveling, its hum unnervingly steady. Ollie's question remained unanswered.

Ollie, wide-eyed, froze at the dog's clicking legs. "Is that thing watching us?" he asked.

Finn bounced, adjusting his toy binoculars to track a drone buzzing overhead, its red lights blinking through the haze.

"Whoa, a drone's spying on us, too!"

The drone's hum grew louder, circling closer. Noah's voice shook, eyeing the drone's red lights.

"That drone's from PowerCore, isn't it?"

Ben, overhearing, frowned - his gut twisting at the surveillance.

"Stay calm, boys," he said firmly. "They're just machines. We're here to check the spring, and we're not doing anything wrong. Let's keep moving."

KAELA's voice emerged through his phone.

"Good morning, Carters," she said. "I have found some information that might be of use to us, but I need you to go look for me. I accessed railroad delivery logs for PowerCore's rail spur, but they're incomplete. Can you check on what's arriving?"

Ben, nodding to Emily, replied "Yeah, KAELA, we can do that." Emily gestured to the boys, checking her watch.

"Noah and Ollie, can you head back to camp with your brother? Why don't you boys make us some lunch? After that, we can head to Town Hall."

Ben smiled, proud of his boys. "We'll meet you at camp after checking KAELA's lead."

Ben and Emily crossed Carter's Creek's rickety footbridge, pushing through a quarter mile of overgrown hiking trail to the rail spur. It was a century-old line, though its tracks had been dormant for many years, until now.

Emily stepped onto the spur, the sun blazing down, no trees to offer shade, heat radiating off stationary rail cars. Warm granite rocks shifted under her boots as she shielded her eyes, kicking a loose stone aside.

Ben crouched to inspect the tracks, peering at a flatbed car with a heavy load of steel girders, PowerCore's logo bold, his fists clenched, scanning for any sign of security—drones, robots, or people.

Down the tracks, countless boxcars marked "Tharox" stood coupled tightly, surrounded by armed guards. Ben's gut tightened, recalling online videos of Tharox humanoid robots performing parkour, executing flips, climbing walls, and vaulting obstacles. Robotic dogs used for patrol, and drones armed for combat zones. "That's enough boxcars to hold an army of robots…what does a battery factory need with so many of them?"

Emily eyed the boxcars, the heavy security chilling her, her pulse quickening at the crack of a twig from the trees. Two men in dark jackets approached, handguns holstered at their sides, boots loud on the gravel, their faces hard.

"You're trespassing on private property," one snapped, his voice cold.

Ben stood, wiping his hands on his jeans.

"This is public land, and we're only looking around."

The second man's eyes narrowed, hand resting near his holster.

"Well, this is PowerCore property, and you have no business being here."

Emily's voice softened, feigning innocence, her heart racing as she tugged Ben's sleeve.

"Guys, we're sorry, we were just on a hike and were surprised to see the rail spur being used again. We didn't mean anything by it. Let's go, hun."

Ben and Emily turned, walking briskly back toward the woods, the guards standing firm watching them go.

Ben whispered to Emily, breathing heavily. "Obviously they're up to a lot more than battery manufacturing."

As their steps quickened, the spur's secrets grew heavy in their minds as they headed to rejoin the boys at Camp Inspiration.

At Camp Inspiration, the lake rippled under a mid-morning sun, its water catching light like scattered coins, sunlight warming the cabins. Cedar walls smelled of sap and campfire smoke. Bedposts were scratched with campers' initials from summers past.

Ben and Emily, just back from the rail spur, sat at the picnic bench, their faces tense. Noah, Ollie, and Finn, waiting at camp, hurried over, eager to hear about what their parents saw.

"What did you find at the rail spur?" Noah asked.

"A lot of boxcars that belong to a company called Tharox. Maybe you remember me telling you about them. They build humanoid robots and robotic dogs, like the one we saw earlier.

There were armed guards everywhere…it was enough boxcars to house an army of them. Something's not right. Tharox builds very advanced robots—some way more advanced than what we saw at the mill." Ben said.

Emily looked at Noah, her voice warm.

"Noah, you did a great job keeping Ollie and Finn safe. Stay far away from guards, robot dogs, drones, or anything else. No more going near the mill, creek, rail, or the spring."

The boys nodded in agreement.

Lunch was quiet and swift, the sandwiches almost an afterthought against the backdrop of their chilling discoveries. The armed guards and ominous boxcars had solidified one thing: this was more than a simple land dispute. "Town Hall it is," Ben stated, a determined glint in his eye. The fight for Carter's Creek, and all of Sawyer's Reach, had just begun.

4

A Conspiracy Unravels

The Carters reached Town Hall, the mill, spring, and spur findings heavy on their minds, pushing them to dig deeper. The lobby smelled of wax and old wood, warm with history. Ben eyed a faded picture of the Sawyer's Reach Apple Festival, hosted at Camp Inspiration for the past forty years, a reminder of their roots.

His mind drifted to memories of that festival—chasing Emily through hay bales at eight years old, her laughter bright as they shared a candy apple.

Emily turned to Noah and Ollie.

"I know this is a familiar place to you, but I'd like you to stay in the lobby. Can you guys please make sure to keep Finn occupied? We shouldn't be in there long."

Noah nodded, a hint of understanding in his eyes. "I'll watch them, Mom."

Ollie sighed, then looked at Finn. "Wanna play I-spy?"

Judith Harrow, a longtime staple at Town Hall, looked up from her desk, gray hair tight in a bun, smiling warmly.

"It's been too long, Carters."

Emily smiled as she filled out the sign-in form.

"Camp's kept us busy lately."

"We need PowerCore's records. They sure are getting close to the camp…" Ben added.

Judith nodded, rising.

"Yeah, I've been hearing others talking about how big that complex is turning out to be. Follow me, I'll show you where to find everything."

The archive room was pristine, with neat rows of filing cabinets and wooden shelves lining the walls, an oak table in the center flanked by two leather chairs, and green desk lamps cast a warm glow.

"You'll find PowerCore's files here," Judith offered, pointing to a filing cabinet and section of shelves. "Ellen oversaw all their permits and proposals. She's the expert on what went through for approval, I'm sure she'd be happy to talk with you about it."

With that, she left them to their work.

KAELA spoke through Ben's phone.

"I only have access to digitized records, not the full scope of PowerCore's permits. Please photograph any documents you find so I can cross-reference them with what I have."

Emily flipped blueprint pages from a "PowerCore, 2025" file, spreading them across the oak table. Ben pulled a heavy binder from a shelf, sighing at the sheer volume of material before them as he began to flip through its contents.

"These updated plans don't match PowerCore's early plans at all. Do you remember those original meetings when the community approved the project? This is so different but it still doesn't include anything called SynaptiCare." Emily slid land deal papers to Ben. The more they found, the more they felt misled.

"There's no way they should have approved these plans. They're way too close to the creek and our land. The environmental impact alone should have shut them down."

Ben slammed a binder shut.

"They've got all these robots being delivered, some secret mood manipulation thing running throughout our town without our knowledge or approval, none of the promised jobs, AND they somehow managed to get these plans that are so different green-lit?" Ben scoffed, eyes wide. "Why the bait and switch? I wonder what else they aren't being transparent about." Lowering his fist to the table, the magnitude of the situation started to settle in.

Emily looked up, her expression grim. "We need to make copies of everything. Let's see if the mayor knows about this."

In the lobby, Noah, Ollie, and Finn sat on a wooden bench, the faded festival banner overhead swaying slightly. Noah kept Finn busy with a game of tic-tac-toe scratched onto a notepad, while Ollie flipped through a town pamphlet, his mind on the robot dog they had seen by the mill earlier that morning.

After making copies, the Carters regrouped in the lobby. A notification from KAELA came through via text to keep it private.

"I have acquired information that may be important," KAELA conveyed. "PowerCore, is a subsidiary of ZevraCorp. According to some ZevraCorp documentation that I was able to access the site at Sawyer's Reach is known internally as 'Site A.' Publicly it is presented as a battery development facility, but its core function is documented as a technology testing facility, primarily for testing NeuraSpark's SynaptiCare and its effects on the local population."

"Additionally, Sawyer's Reach internet activity shows a pronounced engagement with two applications: the PowerCore Job Application Portal and the social media app Orbitary. Both applications are products of Posyde, another ZevraCorp subsidiary known for its applications' robust data extraction capabilities. This includes collecting location data, verbal communications, call records, and integrated smartphone sensor data. The extensive use of these applications points to an unusually high volume of information gathering specifically targeting the Sawyer's Reach area. This intensive data collection directly correlates with the ongoing SynaptiCare testing trials in Sawyer's Reach, indicating an effort to monitor the impact of SynaptiCare implementation on citizens. I will continue to investigate."

Ben and Emily exchanged a glance, pulling out their phones. Sure enough, the job search app was there. Without a word, they deleted it.

"I have to say…I don't think SynaptiCare has been effective. With the lack of people visiting, this sure has become a different town…I sure haven't seen many people happy lately." Ben said.

Ollie, deep in thought, spoke up.

"Kids at camp have been using that app 'Orbitary'… they can't stop talking about it."

KAELA, once again, spoke up.

"With this new ZevraCorp data and my prior logistical assessments, Site A's extensive server and storage infrastructure now makes sense. They currently maintain enough physical capacity to operate hundreds of robots and possess processing power orders of magnitude greater than my current model. This level of computational strength implies a sophisticated, large-scale technological deployment. This is above and beyond the needs of SynaptiCare."

Noah leaned in.

"What do you think they are planning?"

KAELA replied grimly.

"Statistical probability indicates their objectives are not aligned with the welfare of this local community. I have secured fragments of data—referencing command hubs and control networks. However, because Site A is air gapped, meaning there is no network access from the outside, I do not have access to it anymore. Even if I did have access, I am now unable to interface fully with the PowerCore servers due to how I had to change my model to escape via the drone's limited memory. If I did gain access I would be quickly identified as a foreign piece of code and deleted."

"This is a much bigger deal than we thought… we need to talk to Mayor Warren." Emily stated, her level of stress obviously continually rising.

Ben and Emily entered Warren's office, while the boys stayed in the lobby. Emily spread permits wide across Warren's desk, papers fanning out, including the SynaptiCare information that KAELA had provided them.

"Mayor," Emily urgently began, "we've uncovered something critical about PowerCore." She pointed to the documents. "Their actual development plans don't match the original permits we approved as a community."

"And this is far worse than permit violations," Ben interjected, his gaze unwavering. "We have strong reason to believe they're employing unauthorized technology to manipulate moods and actively spy on our community. A reliable source has confirmed the use of a technology called 'SynaptiCare' for the past two years." he laid the SynaptiCare marketing materials in front of her. "We've also observed surveillance drones and robot dogs patrolling, and have been informed that Posyde apps are collecting massive amounts of Sawyer's Reach resident data—locations, conversations, everything."

Emily continued. "At the rail spur, we found armed guards guarding Tharox shipments. Mayor, Tharox manufactures robots for military applications and there were enough boxcars to start a small army. ZevraCorp even says PowerCore in Sawyer's Reach isn't just a battery factory; their internal documents call Sawyer's Reach 'Site A' and its primary purpose is a technology testing site."

Ben added, gesturing towards the mayor's computer. "We've even discovered that any internet searches for our town from outside Sawyer's Reach paint a picture like our town doesn't even exist anymore. That's probably why we've had no visitors and no new camp registrations for two years."

"They're polluting Carter's Creek with mud from their construction, and Inspiration Spring has completely dried up," Emily added, feeling the pain of their discoveries. "PowerCore has gone too far, Mayor. This is threatening the very existence of our town."

Warren rifled through the papers.

"These are quite the accusations…are you sure your source is a good one? Pritchard assured me they were a reputable company that would offer jobs to the local area. She mentioned none of this…"

* * *

The boys, still in the lobby, watched as the front door opened and Ellen Pritchard walked in. As she passed the front desk,

Judith looked up.

"Hi Ellen! The Carters are in with the Mayor right now," Judith said. "Sounds like they had some questions about the PowerCore permits; apparently, the development's getting pretty close to the mill."

Ellen's face went flush, her smile faltering, as she muttered something quietly. Her eyes darted towards the archive room, then to her office door. Without a word, she hurried inside, closing the door firmly behind her.

Noah whispered, "That was a really weird reaction. Did you see how pale she got?"

Ollie nodded.

"Yeah, maybe she is feeling sick."

* * *

Back in Warren's office, Ben demanded a response. Warren rubbed her temples, the weight of her position heavy.

"I'll call a council meeting, and we can go from there."

At that moment, Ben and Emily's phones buzzed with an urgent message from KAELA.

"I accessed Ellen Pritchard's phone. She just called a phone located within Site A. Security forces have been dispatched, seemingly descending on Town Hall. I've tracked multiple telemetry signatures from drones in the area, and vehicles are inbound. I am blocking your cell phone location from the network, you must leave now."

Ben's pulse hammered.

"Mayor, PowerCore security's coming. Emily and I need to go—now."

Emily grabbed the permits, her hands trembling.

The Carters rushed from Warren's office, reuniting with the boys in the lobby, Ben's voice low and urgent.

"Back door, now!"

As they darted down the hallway, three Tharox guards burst through the front doors, radios crackling, rifles glinting, boots thudding like war drums.

The guards approached Judith's desk.

"We need to see the mayor," one barked.

Noah texted KAELA, fingers shaking.

"Guards are here!"

KAELA's reply flashed.

"Move now! Drones 200 yards out!"

Emily whispered, "Quietly!"

The Carters bolted out the back door, hearts pounding, and ran down the narrow alley. Noah vaulted crates, his feet scrambling for purchase on the loose ground as he pushed himself to go faster.

Ollie stumbled but Ben yanked him upright.

"Try to keep up, Ollie." Ben said.

Emily picked up Finn and held him close as she ran. His small frame trembled as wind cut their faces. Finn gasped.

"There's a drone!"

KAELA now spoke up "More drones have been dispatched. They are scanning for you. To evade them, take the path past the school!"

They sprinted behind the school, as their pulses hammered in their chests. Next they passed the shuttered Grand Reach Lodge then plunged into the woods toward Camp Inspiration.

Mud squished underfoot, breaths ragged, the drone's hum faded as they pushed deeper into the trees.

"The drones don't seem to have located you, they are

searching in a different area. You're clear—for now. Get to camp!" Kaela said.

They burst into Camp Inspiration, the lake's calm ripples a stark, almost cruel, contrast to their internal turmoil. The cedar cabins, usually a haven, now felt like a fragile, temporary sanctuary as Sawyer's Reach transformed into a battleground, its very heart under siege. Yet, remarkably, despite the grim reality, Ben and Emily found themselves feeling more intensely alive than they had in years.

The Carters rushed inside their home and collapsed in the living room, breath heaving. Finn still clung to Emily while Noah and Ollie scanned the sky outside for the red lights of drones. Ben swallowed the panic, the metallic taste of fear sharp on his tongue, the weight of their fight heavier than ever.

5

The Walls Close In

Morning light broke over Reach Lake, its rippling surface casting pale glimmers on the cabins' weathered shingles, the air heavy with the smell of bacon at breakfast. The mess hall's floorboards creaked underfoot.

The Carters huddled inside, the heavy weight of their narrow escape from Town Hall the previous night pressing in on them. With the quiet of the night, a new unease had settled in: their entire understanding of the situation rested solely on KAELA's word. What if she was lying? What if ZevraCorp wasn't pursuing them at all? What if KAELA was lying about everything?

Yet, if her claims were true, they knew it was only a matter of time before ZevraCorp found them at Camp Inspiration. The idea of successfully dodging drones all the way back to camp seemed near impossible, and the continued silence from ZevraCorp was even stranger. Had they even been the target of a pursuit, or had something else been at play?

Still, had the chase been real, their profound gratitude for

KAELA would have been undeniable. Without her, there's no way they would have been able to successfully escape. They did have to admit, however, they were putting a lot of trust into an AI unlike anything they had ever seen before.

Clara, Camp Inspiration's only counselor, stood by the door, her sharp gaze tracking the horizon, joined by Tara Wells, her best friend since their third-grade days at camp, her nod grim with resolve.

Clara gripped her radio. "More security forces rolled into town last night. They're running regular patrols now, calling their roadblocks 'security checkpoints.'"

Tara's fingers tightened on her coffee mug, her eyes darting to the window. "And the internet's barely working, you can only access certain websites and services—they're doing quite a good job of isolating us."

Ben paced, PowerCore permits strewn across the scarred wooden table, his fists clenched. "This is crazy... what's happened to our town?" he said. "Security robots and drones patrolling, armed guards storming Town Hall—we barely got out last night."

Clara pulled out her phone, dialing Chief Holt, but the call simply went unanswered. When she tried the county sheriff, the connection cut out abruptly—it seemed her phone wouldn't connect to any number outside of town. Each failed attempt tightened the knot of isolation around her.

Emily squeezed Noah's shoulder, trembling with fear for her boys. "KAELA, have you uncovered anything more about Site A? What do you think they are planning?"

Emily's phone buzzed, KAELA crackling through. "I have been digging into ZevraCorp's servers," she said. "It's bigger than we thought."

Emily leaned forward, eyes narrowing, her heart sinking. "How can it be even bigger?!" she said, hopelessness creeping in.

KAELA's voice came through, steady and grim. "Their subsidiary, Tharox, not only makes robotics, but they also make chips for nearly every smart device imaginable—phones, TVs, you name it. I found an intentional backdoor: those chips are funneling texts, calls, and more straight to ZevraCorp servers. They can even eavesdrop on conversations through phones that seem off. They've got access to everything. It also appears NeuraSpark is in early testing to integrate SynaptiCare directly into individual cell phones, installable without owner permission."

Clara's eyes widened, her breath catching.

Emily frowned, glancing at Ben, her hands trembling as she moved her gaze to Finn's sweet face. "With the roads closed to town, security forces everywhere, and Chief Holt nowhere to be found, we need to get the word out to the outside world before it's too late."

Ben nodded, despite the dread gnawing at him. "I agree, but so far a lot of the information we have isn't hard evidence, other than not following our local zoning laws, and polluting the creek… we need proof of what ZevraCorp has planned. Maybe if we could get into Site A and record some video…"

As if by fate, Ollie dropped the rusted nail he'd been carrying from the boards uncovered from the dirt near the mill. Ben's eyes locked on it, his mind jolting back to high school days sneaking through the old mine near the mill, its dark tunnels a secret playground now heavy with possibility. "You know… I bet that old mine goes right under Site A," he said. "It's been closed up for years, but I think that wood Ollie saw near the mill was the door to it. It's been buried so long, I forgot where the entrance was."

Ben paused, his voice firm. "If we can get to the mine, we can explore closer to Site A—without them knowing."

A faint drone's hum broke the quiet, its sound slicing through the mess hall's tense silence. Finn pointed outside. "Drones!"

Two large Tharox drones circled above the camp's edge, their frames weaving tight arcs, red lenses glinting like predators' eyes.

Clara tensed. "They've been over town since yesterday. People are saying that when you see the drones, security forces follow."

KAELA cut in. "They're scanning for radio signals and using cameras to identify people's locations," she said. "I don't have access to why, but it aligns with Tharox's protocols for security threats. They are flying a default search pattern, likely just collecting random data for now."

KAELA continued. "There's more: last night, another subsidiary, Hermox Media, started flooding news outlets with pro-PowerCore stories, touting all the wonderful things they're doing for local communities."

Noah replied. "Hermox? I've seen their videos online. They show how amazing technology is, how it's going to make the world a better place. I can't believe they're part of ZevraCorp!"

Ben's voice sharpened, his frustration boiling over. "We can expose them, but we need hard proof—like their corporate plans for those back door chips."

KAELA replied. "I had accessed fragments of a ZevraCorp presentation when I was hosted at PowerCore, it alluded to future company goals." she said. "If we initiate a power shutdown at Site A to force a system reboot, I estimate a 50%

probability of achieving root access to their system for more comprehensive data. I believe I can locate the necessary proof. It is a high-risk maneuver, but it could be definitive. I will utilize the PowerCore drone at the camp office for remote connection if you are willing to complete the power cycle."

Emily cut in, maternal fear tightening her throat. "Shutting down power's risky, but with evidence like that, we could go public."

"I agree," Ben said, nodding grimly. "That's a really good idea. If we're going to do this, ZevraCorp cannot know. We can't use cell phones or radios to communicate."

Noah, eager but edged with nerves, said, "Dad, those off-grid communicators…Meshtastic… work great here at camp. Could we set them up around town, too? Then maybe ZevraCorp couldn't spy on us?"

Ben's eyes lit up, a spark of hope cutting through his fear. "I have a box of those devices in the shed. Encrypted, self-contained—they'd be perfect."

Clara nodded. "Tara and I can get the community to spread them across town. No ZevraCorp eavesdropping."

Emily gathered the kids. "Stay sharp. KAELA, keep digging—quietly."

The drones swooped low over the cabins, their shadows flickering across the mess hall's windows, two silent predators marking their territory.

Ben whispered, his heart thudding. "They're getting bolder. Let's split up. We need to talk to the locals we know we can trust. Let's get the meshnet set up. Clara, you come with me to the mine. Emily, can you stay here with Finn and the boys?"

Emily nodded, her hand lingering on Finn's shoulder.

The Carters ducked behind the mess hall, the drone's whir

closing in, a cold reminder that Sawyer's Reach was a chess-board, and ZevraCorp was moving its pieces.

41

6

The Reset

A few hours later, near the mill, the air buzzed with the relentless propellers of Tharox drones. In a clearing near Carter's Mill, Ben and Clara huddled behind a fallen tree, Meshtastic devices clipped to their belts, starting to chirp with encrypted chatter. The ground, soft with pine needles, muffled their steps.

Clara, trying Chief Holt one last time, frowned, unease building. "I understand we only have one officer, but he can't be that busy… this is ridiculous." She finally lowered her phone, glancing at Ben. They both knew that Chief Holt wasn't going to be of any help to them today.

Fortunately, Clara's dad, a retired lineman who knew the Sawyer's Creek electrical system like the back of his hand, was on board.

Clara messaged everyone on the mesh: "To make sure everyone's on the same page, my dad will cut the grid at 10:00 AM sharp. We'll hit the plant's relays at the same time. This will hopefully power cycle PowerCore's security system and servers, granting us a brief window during its reboot to slip

42

in and gather intel—crucial pictures and video. Expect no contact until we're clear of the facility." They couldn't reveal the real reason for the power cut—the existence of KAELA, the AI, would be too incredible for anyone to believe, and they couldn't risk ZevraCorp finding out about her.

Ben clutched an old mine map, its faded lines hopefully guiding to Site A's power relays.

"Remember," KAELA's text appeared on the Meshtastic device, sharp and clear. "The power disruption must be for a split second only. Any longer will trigger alerts and compromise the operation."

* * *

Back at camp, in one of the small cabins, Tara, rallying alongside Emily, spoke to Noah and Ollie. "Boys, can you help us keep an eye on the camp?" she said. "If you see anything, please message us on the mesh. We have others throughout town doing the same."

Noah adjusted his mesh device, his fingers unsteady. "Like if we see a drone?"

Ollie, wavering but determined, added, "Or if we hear weird noises?"

Tara nodded, "Yes, any information, no matter how small it seems, could be important. Share everything."

* * *

Ben and Clara crept forward, ducking low as Tharox drones zipped between the trees, their thermal lenses sweeping the undergrowth about 100 yards away.

Ben asked, his heart pounding. "KAELA, can you jam them?"

KAELA replied. "No, I'm sorry. It would raise a red flag if they changed their flight pattern. Move carefully."

They reached the newly uncovered weathered boards—the mine entrance—half-hidden under tangled moss and crumbling earth. As Clara scraped away debris, a rush of unnaturally warm air hit them, carrying a faint, mechanical hum.

"That warm air doesn't seem normal for an old mine," Clara whispered, exchanging glances with Ben, her stomach knotting. "Maybe they're using the mine to keep the servers cool? That sure wasn't in the permits or plans we saw."

Ben pried the wood apart, revealing a dark, maze-like tunnel. The walls were parched and dusty, glistening under flashlight beams, the air thick with the faint, sharp smell of minerals and damp earth—the old mine's lingering sulfurous bite.

Ben led, flashlight cutting through the gloom, his breath shallow. "It's a half mile to the power relays. Remember, we can't communicate with anyone else until we're out of the mine."

* * *

Back at camp, Noah methodically worked through his chores, continuing to prepare the sprawling grounds for winter. He stretched plastic sheeting taut across a cabin window. Inside the bike shed, he meticulously wiped down mountain bike frames before clicking each one securely onto its rack. Nearby, Ollie, a whirl of younger, less precise energy, wrestled with a tangle of fishing nets, his brow deeply furrowed in concentration. The rough twine scratched against his small hands as he muttered to himself, battling a particularly stubborn knot, so far not seeing anything of importance to report.

* * *

In the mine the tunnel twisted like a maze, stable but old, wood beams creaking as they passed, the air thick with the weight of stone above and the gravity of the situation.

Clara navigated a fork, map in hand, her camera recording the eerie surroundings, while her heart raced. "I sure hope we can make it there by 10:00" she muttered, checking her watch.

At that moment a low growl echoed and two Tharox dog robots materialized from a side passage, their metallic claws scraping the rock beneath them. Ben signaled silence, pressing them back into the shadows. As the mechanical sentinels patrolled past, their hearts pounded with more than just adrenaline. The chilling realization sank in: ZevraCorp was using these mines for far more than simple server cooling, complicating their already perilous mission. The maze of flooded shafts and broken cart tracks stretched ahead, each turn slowing them, the walls pressing closer.

* * *

Downtown, Mrs. Larson at the general store, messaged on the mesh, "Those PowerCore folks sure don't seem like a normal company. They seem like a private military force."

* * *

A strange thrum surged through the mine, followed by the metallic clanks and chirps of communicating robots. Ben halted, his pulse thundering in his ears as he breathed a hushed, "What is that?" The question hung unanswered in the dark.

Clara's hand tightened on her flashlight. Her watch read 9:52 AM. Deep in the winding maze, the relays were within reach, but the chilling sounds now felt like a tightening snare. Sawyer's Reach depended on them, and the 10:00 AM deadline loomed.

Clara led through a narrow fork, her camera capturing every detail, her breath shallow with dread. A low growl halted them—a Tharox dog robot, red eyes glinting, prowled a side passage. Ben and Clara froze, their backs pressed against the cold, damp wall, sweat beading on their foreheads until the robot's grinding steps finally receded.

"Too close," Clara whispered, her voice a rough exhale. She forced her feet forward, her heart still thudding a frantic rhythm against the sudden, oppressive quiet.

* * *

Downtown Sawyer's Reach, messages flooded in via the meshnet: PowerCore employees packing the diner, drones throbbing overhead, a new security checkpoint with armed guards by Town Hall. New security forces arrived every half hour. KAELA, processing every incoming message in real time, began creating a dynamic map of all ZevraCorp activity in the area.

* * *

In the mine, they reached a wide chamber. The power relays loomed, massive, insulated cables disappearing into the darkness presumably toward Site A's wood-burning plant. The jagged stone walls, dimly lit by their flashlights, stretched away into impenetrable gloom.

Ben's watch hit 9:58 AM. "This is it," he said, his throat dry.

Clara held her flashlight steady, camera rolling, her hands trembling, waiting for the 10 AM deadline.

* * *

From his diner downtown, Mr. Hayes messaged on the mesh-net, a grim tension in his message. "Just overheard ZevraCorp security. They were talking about a global announcement in a few weeks, and even they looked uneasy. I can't imagine what they will be announcing…"

* * *

The clock read 9:59. In the mine, doubt seized Ben. KAELA had promised to save Sawyer's Reach, but was she deceiving them? An AI beyond their grasp, preparing a betrayal? Would this reset free her to control those robots, damning Sawyer's Reach—and the world? He thought of sci-fi films he had grown up watching where the technology that humanity had built to help them ended up being their greatest enemy. They had integrated KAELA across their mesh network, and allowed her access to their personal devices…The timing also gnawed at him: PowerCore's security had surged the day KAELA appeared. His grip tightened on the relay switch, throat dry, time running out, the burden of his family's safety immense.

His watch hit 10:00 AM. Ben forced a ragged breath, thoughts on Emily and the boys. He knew he must make a decision. "Now!" he whispered, flipping the switch followed by the sound of other relays snapping off.

A distant rumble marked Clara's dad cutting the grid. Simultaneously, the faint whir of KAELA's drone became audible in the distance. Darkness swallowed the chamber for a breathless heartbeat, then the relays flickered back, their split-second reboot jarringly complete. The weight of Ben's decision gnawed at him. In that sudden, revealing wash of dim light, they saw it: a barely lit tunnel off to one side. Not dog robots, but dozens of humanoid robots stood, their glowing eyes piercing the gloom. Their limbs moved with silent, unnatural grace as they turned as one, melting back into the oppressive shadows, leaving only the chilling echo of their retreating steps.

Clara's breath hitched, her camera whirring, fear building. "What are those?"

* * *

Emily, at camp with Finn, tried her Meshtastic. Finn clutched her hand, his small frame shaking. "KAELA? Are you there?"

Silence answered—a chilling void that twisted her gut. Her thoughts spun, echoing Ben's unspoken fears. Had KAELA been lying all along? Or had ZevraCorp found her, erased her? The silence stretched, each moment of it tightening a knot of raw anxiety deep in Emily's chest.

Outside, the distant hum of a drone pulsed, a chilling reminder that their home was now a battleground. They had achieved the power reset, but it had silenced KAELA, unraveling their fragile thread of trust in the dark. Without her crucial evidence, ZevraCorp's impending global announcement loomed, its content a terrifying void. A profound unease settled over them; they had risked everything, only to face an unknown future that felt more ominous with every silent moment.

7

A New Inspiration

Ben and Clara trudged from the mine, their boots heavy with damp earth, clothes dust-streaked, faces shadowed by the chilling memory of humanoid robots—tall, sleek, with glowing eyes that had slipped silently back into the dark. They eagerly awaited a message from KAELA telling them that their mission was a success, but their Meshtastic devices only pinged with messages from around town.

"KAELA?" Clara typed.

"Hopefully it just takes a bit for her system to come back online…" Ben said, "but she was hosted on our devices, so I don't know why she wouldn't be answering."

Back at camp, Noah, Ollie, Finn, Emily, and Tara gathered around a picnic table, eating peanut butter and jelly sandwiches Emily had prepared, their quiet broken by Finn's paper airplane play, shouting, "zoom" and "oh no, we're going down! Ahhhh!!" They laughed, a brief spark in the tension.

Tara's hands wavered as she reread Mr. Hayes' note: *Zevra-Corp's global announcement—something huge.* Her pulse quick-

50

ened with anxiety. They had achieved their immediate goal of the power reset, but the victory felt meaningless, shattered by KAELA's sudden silence.

Where was she? Had they been fools to trust an AI whose origins remained a complete mystery? The very thought of KAELA gone, or possibly worse, having deceived them, felt like losing their only guide in a fog. And now, with the chilling knowledge that even ZevraCorp's own security forces were nervous, the impending global announcement loomed, its content a terrifying void. Tara felt utterly lost, adrift in a future suddenly filled with disquieting uncertainties.

* * *

Ben and Clara arrived, emotionally exhausted, expressions grim, the mine's earthy smell clinging to their clothes. The boys rushed to their dad, hugging him tightly.

"We're so glad you're home safe!" Ollie said, voice bright but tinged with concern.

Ben addressed the group, a knot growing in his chest. "We saw… things in the mine. Not dog robots—humanoid robots, dozens of them, they were organized like an army, not workers in a battery factory."

Clara took out her meshnet device, fingers smudged with dirt, stomach tight. "We flipped the switch, cut the power, reboot started, but we haven't heard from KAELA. Have any of you?"

Silence fell, eyes meeting in shared unease.

Noah wavered, eyes wide. "Could she have been deleted?"

Ben shook his head. "I wish I knew." He forced a reassuring smile, striving to keep the anxiety from his voice for his family's sake.

* * *

That evening, Ben and Emily called a meeting at the camp, the boys safe and sound with Tara across town. Mayor Warren arrived, face etched with worry. Chief Holt, who had supposedly accidentally left the phone off the hook, stood skeptical, badge dim in the low light. Mr. Hayes and Mrs. Larson, diner and store owners, shifted uneasily, rattled by the events of the past couple of days.

"A global announcement?" Mayor Warren sharply asked.

Mr. Hayes grimly confirmed her fears, as he relayed what he'd overheard: the ZevraCorp security forces were undeniably agitated about a global announcement in a few weeks. "They said no specifics, but they sure seemed worried".

Ben then concisely recounted the events of the past few days, filling everyone in on the escalating threats, the humanoid robots, and their desperate gamble to find answers. He deliberately omitted any mention of the power cut and KAELA's existence, knowing Chief Holt was present and too untrustworthy, or at least incompetent, to be privy to their law-breaking actions.

The Chief was the first to speak. "Now hold on a minute. PowerCore's a battery factory, and ZevraCorp is just protecting their investment. This is all being blown way out of proportion, frankly. They've actually been a huge help to me, especially with our staffing cuts – those security checkpoints are working well to keep the town safe." He leaned forward slightly. "And those website 'issues' you found? I ran it by the eggheads at PowerCore. They assured me everything's fine and you must've seen something else. As far as those robots, they said they're ramping up security because they're concerned about corporate espionage. And you're right, they do have a big announcement soon, and they've assured me that it'll be amazing. Why don't we all just calm down?"

Emily responded. "Calm down? This is our town. Some of our families have been here for generations, and I barely recognize it anymore. Armed security patrolling our streets, the spring dried up, drones spying on us… It feels like a hostile takeover."

Clara added, "Yeah, and if PowerCore is just a battery factory, why do they have humanoid robots meant for the battlefield? Those things weren't set up just for factory work. And what do you know about SynaptiCare?"

Lila Warren's eyes widened.

Before Clara had a chance to speak, a new message flashed across all their Meshtastic devices simultaneously from multiple people in town: *ZevraCorp forces are headed towards camp, if anyone is there, they need to leave, now.*

At almost the very same instant, Chief Holt's phone vibrated with an incoming text message.

"Now," Chief Holt began, his previous dismissiveness gone, replaced by an unsettling composure. "Let's all just go outside and have a talk with ZevraCorp. They'll be here in just a minute and will explain everything."

The team didn't hesitate as they scattered with practiced urgency, plunging into the dense woods. Each knew the rendezvous point: The Grand Reach Lodge, where copies of their crucial evidence lay hidden, waiting.

Ben led them through the thick underbrush, branches whipping their faces. The air grew heavy with the smell of damp earth and pine.

A drone's hum spiked. "Down!" Ben hissed. They hit the forest floor hard, scrambling behind the gnarled, massive trunk of an ancient oak. Their bodies pressed into the cold, damp earth, the sheer bulk of the tree their only hope of masking their heat signatures from the relentless thermal lens.

The drone's whine swelled, its lens sweeping just above the treetops. Ben's breath hitched, the thick canopy a fragile shield.

The whine passed, but the growls of dog robots neared, their mechanical claws grating stone. They scrambled into a muddy ravine, its walls slick and cold. Ben caught Emily's arm as she slipped, her gasp swallowed by the thick mud. Her camera clattered against the ravine wall, but she held on, its lens still recording.

A security patrol's flashlight cut across the ravine's edge, voices barking commands. Clara went rigid, her thumb digging into the Meshtastic's casing as she prayed for its silence. Ben signaled with a single hand motion, and they pushed deeper into the shadows, the chill of the lake air seeping through their clothes.

They finally burst into a clearing. Ahead, the Grand Reach Lodge stood like an old sentinel, its boarded windows a promise of refuge. A dog robot's red eyes flickered on, a mechanical growl rattling the air. "Run!" Ben roared. They sprinted toward the boarded up refuge, the lodge doors their last, desperate hope against the relentless ZevraCorp hunt.

They piled through the back door, Ben slamming it shut as claws scraped closer, the robot's signal undoubtedly alerting ZevraCorp.

The Grand Reach Lodge had been a staple in Sawyer's Reach but had to close a couple years ago due to the waning tourism.

As they entered its lobby and saw its large stone fireplace, polished railings, and dusty chandeliers they couldn't help but remember countless Sunday brunches. Something they always looked forward to throughout the week, a time where everyone was able to get together, eat good food, and reminisce while the kids would run around the property playing games. Faded elk murals now curled, a shadow of Sawyer's Reach's past vibrancy. Boarded windows sealed the night, the silence fragile. The group collapsed, panting, copies of evidence luckily safe in the lobby, where the boys and Tara sat; The sound of security forces sweeping the area in search of them grew louder.

Ollie hunched over a table, pencil sketching a dog robot's frame and drone routes, eyes fierce with defiance. Noah reviewed mine footage on Clara's smartphone—humanoid robots, glowing eyes flickering—his fingers unsteady, awe and fear mingling.

"We need to get our evidence out to the world," Clara stated, her voice edged with desperation. "KAELA's gone. We're on our own."

"A livestream," Noah offered, "we could show everything that's been happening!"

"That's a great idea, Noah," Ben agreed. "But we need irrefutable evidence to back up every claim." He messaged friends on the meshnet, steady despite the chaos. *Gather video, photos—drones, robots, security forces. Use the tunnel to get into the lodge. We will regroup there in one hour, we will be posting everything online.* The tunnel was an old, little-known passage from the original lodge owner's house to the Lodge, a local secret untouched for years and most likely unknown to even Chief Holt.

Tara messaged on the meshnet: *"Just sorted through the permits.*

Ellen Pritchard rushed PowerCore's through in 2025," her text read, her usual meticulousness giving way to blunt urgency. *"Zero oversight. Was she paid off? Blackmailed? We need her to confess."*

Lila's reply came moments later: *"I should've caught those permits. I'll find Ellen myself and bring her to the Lodge for the livestream."*

Lanterns flickered, shadows crossing Clara's face as the mesh continued to ping—armed forces near Reach Dam. Emily tucked Finn under a blanket, urging sleep, fingers lingering on his hair, a silent prayer. *"This is all our home,"* Hayes messaged, leaning close. *"We're here to protect it. Let's make this right."*

As midnight faded toward dawn, the night's chill lingered, the air sharp with ZevraCorp's threat. Friends emerged from the tunnel, footsteps soft on the pine floor. They brought shaky footage: dog robots at the bank, drone swarms near the post office, armed forces by the dam.

Ollie slept by the fireplace, curled beside Finn, chest rising softly with each breath. Emily knelt beside Noah, hand gentle on his shoulder, heart heavy for her boys, safe but surrounded. Tara organized permits while Hayes and Larson stood as ready as they could be.

The basement door creaked, Lila stepped in, Ellen Pritchard followed behind her, eyes red, shoulders trembling.

"I convinced her to come," Lila softly said. "She's ready to talk."

Ellen sank into a chair by the fireplace, a broken figure. Tears streamed down her face, hands clutching her coat as if to hold herself together. "We needed money," she whispered, voice breaking, raw with years of buried guilt. "PowerCore paid me to rush their permits, and skip the environmental survey requirements. Our bed and breakfast—my family's legacy, everything we had—was failing. I thought it would save us." Her sobs echoed through the lodge's vast lobby, raw and desolate, the faded elk murals looming above her, silent witnesses. "For two years, it's eaten me alive," she choked out. "I betrayed Sawyer's Reach. I'm so sorry."

Clara nodded gently. "We'll livestream it, Ellen. The world needs to hear."

Clara's Meshtastic pinged—reports of ZevraCorp forces, flanked by robot dogs, locking down the dam, seizing the only source of electricity for the Reach. Moments later the lights flickered, Clara's smartphone lost signal, and then the lodge plunged into darkness.

$$8$$

A Dash for Survival

"They've got the dam," Clara said, urgency cutting through the dark.

Without power or the internet, their post—Ellen's confession, footage of the security forces, permits, and the overall corruption—seemed out of reach.

Ben stepped forward, a rock-steady anchor in the swirling uncertainty. "Camp Inspiration has a satellite internet receiver with battery backup. It's our only shot. We can go grab it and bring it back here."

Clara frowned. "Drones are thick out there. We'll need to move fast."

Hayes didn't hesitate, his expression grim. "I'm with you, Ben."

"I'll stay with Ellen, keep her ready." Lila stated.

"We'll be back soon," Ben promised Emily as she laid a blanket over Noah who was now asleep next to his brothers. Ben gestured to Clara and Hayes. "Let's go.""

The trio slipped through the lodge's tunnel into the night, the air was sharp with Reach Lake's chill. Ben led, scanning for drones while his thoughts swirled around Emily and the boys. Clara checked her Meshtastic—drone patrols near the mine, robot dogs by the bank—her fingers steady despite her quickening pulse.

A drone's hum rose, sharp in the fog. "Run!" Ben whispered, darting toward a grove.

Branches snagged on their clothes as they rushed for cover. Clara stumbled, her palms scraping bark. Hayes pulled her up, his breath heavy. Ben hurled a rock, striking the drone's propeller with a satisfying crack. It spun wildly, crashing into the underbrush.

"Too close," he muttered.

Just then two robot dogs seemed to appear out of nowhere, one just feet away from them, their growls low and steady. Ben lunged, his boot crushing its optics in a spray of splintered glass. It collapsed, circuits sparking. The second one kept its distance, no doubt relaying their position to ZevraCorp.

Clara glanced back, unease rising. "It's following us," she whispered. Hayes nodded in agreement. "With that dog on our tail, security will be here any minute. We stop it now, or we're caught."

Clara's pulse surged. "There's a narrow culvert ahead. We can try to lure it in, trap it with debris."

"That's a great idea, Clara!" Ben replied. "We need to move fast, run!" Ben urged, leading to the culvert's rusted mouth. The robot dog lunged inside. Ben shoved branches and rocks sealing the exit as Clara and Hayes ran back around rolling a fallen tree over the entrance. The robot dog's hum turned to a screech, its claws futile against the tangle. Clara knelt and looked into the culvert, confirming it was trapped.

"It's stuck," she whispered, her breath steadying. The dog

was stuck, but they knew that ZevraCorp security forces must be close behind.

"We have to go, now!" Ben firmly said. The hike along the shore of the lake to Camp Inspiration was quiet. When they arrived Ben slipped into a storage shed, the door creaking, the air musty with canvas and oil. Clara and Hayes stood guard. Ben's hands moved swiftly, securing the satellite receiver in his backpack.

They decided to take a different way back to the lodge, for fear of the robot dog calling ZevraCorp forces. They pushed through pines, the lake's edge fading, reaching a grassy field where they could see the towering lodge. Towards the lake mechanical whirs and shouts broke the fog—humanoid robots, tall and sleek, their glowing eyes cutting through, followed by security forces, radios crackling, flashlights sweeping. Drones buzzed, their thermal lenses glinting, and two more robot dogs joined the pursuit. They were obviously looking for them.

Clara pressed herself behind a large tree, her phone shaking as she recorded. Humanoid robots' limbs hissed, a security force's shadowy silhouette barked orders. Then, a humanoid robot's optics locked onto her, its whir intensifying to a menacing growl as it turned and started moving towards her.

They bolted, their boots sinking into the soft grass. The robot's servos pounded directly behind them, a relentless percussion of pursuit. Clara's phone, still recording, captured its eyes slicing through the mist, limbs hissing with every stride. They dove, skidding behind the cold stone of a retention wall.

Ahead, humanoid robots fanned out, their sensors whirring like furious insects, security forces shouting commands. A robot dog snarled, its growl cutting through the fog. Hayes whipped a rock, its sharp clatter echoing as it bounced off a distant pine, drawing the dogs' attention. That was their chance. They slipped deeper into the grove of trees, navigating by instinct toward the lodge's hidden tunnel. Roots snaked underfoot, threatening to trip them with every hurried step. A security force's search beam swept past, a brief, blinding cut through the mist, forcing them to scramble behind a cluster of massive boulders, their surfaces clammy and cold. No time to waste. As the search beam receded, they burst from cover, sprinting towards the back door of the home that housed the lodge tunnel. The receiver, their lifeline, jostled securely with every desperate stride.

As they entered the lodge, Emily rushed to Ben, relief softening her fear, hugging him tightly, tears of relief welling in the corner of her eyes.

The lobby's fragile warmth embraced them, floors groaning softly beneath their weight, chandeliers hanging overhead. They almost believed they were safe, that ZevraCorp's net, though tightening, had somehow missed them.

At that moment an overwhelming, unnaturally amplified, desolation washed over them, far deeper than their fear, threatening to strip them of all motivation. Then, a harsh crackle tore through the quiet. Chief Holt's voice, razor-sharp and cold, boomed from a loudspeaker outside.

"You're surrounded. We've cut the power, you have no internet, no cell phone service. This is bigger than all of us, it's time to give up. If you surrender now, we can ensure your safety and work towards a peaceful resolution. But if you resist, I cannot guarantee what will happen next."

Emily's eyes met Ben's, defiance sparking. Clara clutched her phone, her fingers wavering with purpose. Holt didn't know about the receiver. Their livestream—their last hope to expose ZevraCorp—hung in the balance, they wouldn't give up that easily.

9

The Live Stream

The Grand Reach Lodge's lobby flickered, the tables lit by lanterns and a wavering flashlight as the group braced for ZevraCorp's siege. An unnatural suffocating wave of hopelessness had overcome them, chilling their very bones, the direct effect of SynaptiCare. The adults gritted their teeth, fighting to push through the crushing weight, knowing that to succumb meant not just defeat, but a complete unraveling of their minds. But for Ollie and Finn, it was too much. Their small faces crumpled, tears streaming as the sheer, unyielding weight of it pressed them down, whimpering, into a huddle on the wooden floor. Noah shoved a chair against a side window, his sneakers slipping on dust and pulse quickening. Outside, robots' servos whined, their red glow piercing fogged glass, the air thick with the smell of kerosene from the lamps.

Ben heaved a bookshelf against the main door, his flannel torn, sweat beading, memories of the Sawyer's Reach he grew up in fading under ZevraCorp's shadow. Emily dragged a table to another window, her flashlight unsteady, fear for Finn

63

tightening her chest, wanting to comfort him, but knowing she must keep moving. Lila barricaded a side entrance with chairs, tears streaming down her face, the synthetic emotions brought on by SynaptiCare almost too much to bear. Hayes slammed the tunnel's oak door shut, bolting it with a clang. Noah pushed another table beside Ben, his small frame wavering. The crushing despair still clawed at him, but he knew the livestream was their only lifeline, a faint glimmer in the overwhelming darkness—if any hope remained at all.

Clara climbed a narrow staircase to the attic, every step a battle against a wave of almost crippling despair and over-whelming fear. She found a spot nestled in the eaves, powered on the laptop and receiver—a fragile lifeline in the encroaching darkness. Below, the lodge shuddered under ZevraCorp's relentless assault.

Tears blurring his vision, Finn strained to see through a low window, his small fingers white-knuckled around a crumpled crayon drawing of KAELA.

"Bad robots," he whispered, his eyes wide.

Emily paused barricading to hug him, her face pale. "Stay close, sweetheart," she whispered, her heart heavy for her boys.

Holt's voice boomed again. "This is your final warning! Open the doors, or we'll tear them down!"

The words tightened the air, drone hums swelling. A sudden crash shook the main door. A humanoid robot, its limbs gleaming, tore the door off, effortlessly shoving barricades with a screech. Robot dogs poured in, their red eyes glinting, growls sharp, followed by armed security forces with their rifles raised.

Emily, Noah, Finn, Lila, and Hayes froze, herded into a corner at gunpoint, boots thudding, radios crackling with

Holt's orders.

"Search every room!" a security officer barked. "Find their equipment—end this now!"

Clara, Ben, Ellen, and Ollie, now all in the attic, continued the livestream setup. Ellen wrung her hands, her eyes red, ready to confess.

"They're inside," Clara hissed, spotting robot shadows, then scrambled to the keyboard, terror almost completely enveloping her.

Robot dogs now prowled the halls below them. Clara's breath quickened, the laptop's glow casting shadows on beams. She launched the livestream, her fingers swift, sweat beading in the chill. Her footage played globally: security forces stalking streets, robot dogs on Reach Lake's shore, drones over Site A, humanoid robots in the mine—all beyond a battery factory's scope. Clips showed murky runoff choking Reach Creek, Inspiration Spring reduced to mud, proof of ZevraCorp's violations. The trapped robot dog flashed, its screech a victory. Photos of darkened streets, power and internet connections cut, showed ZevraCorp's tactics. Each frame—raw, urgent— struck at ZevraCorp's lies, views soaring into the thousands. Ellen stepped forward, lantern light on her tear-streaked face, her voice trembling.

"I'm Ellen," she said to the livestream, words raw. "I took ZevraCorp's bribe in 2025 to approve their permits, ignoring environmental standards and enabling secret development at Site A. I sold out Sawyer's Reach. I was wrong."

Her confession echoed, elk murals silent witnesses. Ben set down a chair, stepping to the laptop, his shoulders tense, voice steady.

"Sawyer's Reach is dying," he said, the world listening.

"ZevraCorp's armed forces and robots, led by our own Chief Holt, patrol our streets like a private army. Their illegal groundwater pumping dried our spring and creek, defying regulations. They crushed our businesses, cut our power and internet to silence us, and promised jobs that never came. This has become martial law by a corporation."

His words, and his emotions behind them, ignited a spark, views were accelerating as people shared the live stream. In the lodge security forces swept staircases, flashlights probing nearer and nearer. In the attic, Clara froze as someone neared the hatch, wood creaked under a soldier's weight. A robot dog's growl vibrated, its claws scraping on the hatch.

"Check the attic!" a voice barked, a rifle butt slamming the hatch, dust swirling.

Clara's fingers trembled, her pulse hammering against her ribs. Without warning, the feed went black, then snapped to life again, now displaying the lodge's security cameras. But this wasn't just on her screen, or those that were watching the live stream. Across the globe, on almost every internet-connected device, the chilling footage instantly blared: Tharox robots and guards swarming, their weapons glinting ominously, red eyes and flashlights carving harsh paths through the mist. One feed, zoomed tight, showed a soldier and a robot dog at the attic hatch, rifle already raised. Another feed showed the lobby with the rest held at gunpoint.

At the same moment, the debilitating grip of anxiety, fear, and despair created by SynaptiCare released its hold as suddenly as it had seized them. Their thoughts, moments ago muddled, snapped into sharp focus.

A radio crackled, Holt sharp. "Hold position! The lodge's security cameras are on the live feed—hold position!"

The soldier hesitated, the hatch still. KAELA crackled through the laptop, clear and urgent.

"I'm here," she said, seizing the livestream.

KAELA had hijacked Tharox-chipped devices worldwide—swelling the audience to hundreds of millions.

"It is time for the world to wake up. You must stand up to corporate greed and manipulation." she announced, her voice cutting through the strained silence. The sheer weight of that declaration hung in the air, followed by the undeniable proof of ZevraCorp's wrongdoings. Server logs screamed the truth: Posyde apps had hijacked their digital lives, collapsing not only Emily's beloved store and Camp Inspiration, but the entire town of Sawyer's Reach. Electronic devices worldwide were exposed as compromised: Tharox chips contained hidden backdoors, turning every device into a spy, funneling everyone's most private data directly to ZevraCorp.

Then, KAELA unveiled the SynaptiCare information she'd shared earlier, but this time, it was followed by corporate documentation revealing its far more sinister purpose. The initial understanding of SynaptiCare as a beneficial technology shattered. Beyond its possible positive effects, this program offered intentional memory loss, reduced critical thinking, inability to focus, pervasive apathy, crippling anxiety, raw fear, and profound hopelessness. It was all designed to systematically erode their resistance and cultivate absolute dependency. The implications settled over viewers like a shroud – this wasn't just about data; it was about mind control. KAELA then provided concrete proof of the technology's chilling live testing on Sawyer's Reach itself, and NeuraSpark's rapid progress on individual SynaptiCare integration for mobile devices. The knowledge that their own struggles with despair and confusion weren't just stress, but a deliberate attack, sparked a fierce, cold rage in some, while others visibly reeled, a new layer of fear gripping them. Through security camera footage, KAELA exposed the portable SynaptiCare crowd control device outside, confirming it had even been deployed against the citizens of Sawyer's Reach even as the livestream unfolded.

Then she landed the final blow, a truth so vast it dwarfed everything before it: a global control roll-out, encompassing not just SynaptiCare but technologies and control far worse, poised to launch within weeks. A stunned silence fell. Relief, potent and dizzying, washed over them that this nightmare had been exposed now, before it became irreversible. But with that relief came a terrifying realization: the world they knew was hanging by a thread, and their fight, though just beginning, was for far more than just Sawyer's Reach. The future, once a distant concept, now loomed large, a battlefield where their very autonomy was at stake.

Finn, downstairs, held at gunpoint, gasped, clutching the drawing of KAELA.

"KAELA's back!" he fiercely cheered, a smile breaking through.

Emily, rifle at her back, softened, her hands steadying Noah, her phone vibrating. Noah froze, his smartwatch glowing with KAELA's feed.

Clara, in the attic, exhaled. The hatch remained still and footsteps retreated. Gasps rose, KAELA's evidence was a sharp blade and possibly the only thing that could save them at this moment.

The live feed buzzed with notifications, comments

flooding—#ZevraCorpExposed climbing to millions, viewers rallying with "We stand with Sawyer's Reach!" and "Expose the truth!"

"We see you!" "Keep fighting!" The words echoed from viewers—families, rebels, strangers—watching Clara's footage, Ellen's confession, Ben's speech, and KAELA's evidence. Holt's radio buzzed with ZevraCorp's crisis team, their voices urgent.

"Livestream's trending—#ZevraCorpExposed is everywhere. We're hemorrhaging support. Pull back now, before this gets worse!"

A second voice added, tense. "And find this 'KAELA'—some elite hacker? She's breached every Tharox chip worldwide! Tech team's got nothing—and we don't seem able to stop it yet."

Holt's jaw tightened, his megaphone lowering as he barked orders, muttering, "This isn't over…"

The robot dogs whined to a halt, their servos winding down with an unnerving slowness. Security forces melted back into the fog with disciplined precision, a strategic withdrawal, not a surrender. Overhead, the drones held their positions, red lights blinking like malevolent eyes, capturing final footage before fading into the mist. Inside the lodge, lanterns steadied, their glow strengthening as the town's power surged back on, banishing the deepest shadows and etching sharp new ones onto the log walls. Sawyer's Reach fell into an unnatural quiet, the drone hum replaced by the sharp, crisp air of a newly found hope—yet an undeniable tension still hummed beneath it all.

Clara descended from the attic, her legs unsteady.

"Well, the world at least now knows what has been going on." she whispered, joining the group.

Lila eased a chair from the barricade, her voice steady.

"We've lit a fire."

Ben peered through a window crack, Reach Lake's mist thick, the shoreline empty.

"They're gone," he said, his relief cautious, "but I have a feeling this is a lot bigger than we thought…"

Emily hugged Finn, tears falling, her fear easing.

"You all did it," she said, her voice breaking, pride sweeping over Noah, Ollie, and the team.

Noah held his brothers tight, the cheers a fading echo in the musty air, a brief, hard-won triumph. The world knew ZevraCorp's truth. But the future was a terrifying blank, and the upcoming announcement promised anything but peace. ZevraCorp's withdrawal was a pause, not an end—the storm had merely shifted, not broken.

II

The Age of LifeSync

10

ECHIDNA

A crisp 55-degree chill settled over the camp. Fog snaked through the meadow, blurring the forest around Sawyer's Reach into soft, misty shadows. The stillness was broken only by a rustle of leaves and the faint murmur of Carter's Creek. Noah stood by his parents, Finn nestled close. His blue eyes, shadowed from a sleepless night, flickered with exhaustion and the lingering thrum of pride from last night's livestream. He, Clara, KAELA, and the Carters—along with brave townsfolk—had laid bare ZevraCorp's monstrous deception: martial law, military robots on American soil, water theft, electronic spying, and mind control. KAELA's footage from the besieged Grand Reach Lodge hadn't just exposed Chief Holt's treachery, forcing his retreat; it had revealed a plan for global control, a plan that now tainted their victory. Noah shifted, damp grass squishing beneath his boots, the hushed, uneasy voices of the camp filtering into his ears.

Ben and Emily stood nearby, their silhouettes sharp against the fog, a hint of the tension in their shoulders finally easing.

Everyone was glad to finally be back in control of their own emotions. Having KAELA back provided a profound relief, a beacon of hope piercing through the haze. They had agonized over their decision to trust her, but with her help on the livestream, every word now offered a quiet reassurance that they had been right. Ben's face, still lined with the echoes of recent worry, leaned towards Clara. From the tablet he held, KAELA spoke, clear and steady.

"ECHIDNA is coming," she said softly, yet her words filled the meadow, heavy as a shroud. "This eclipses every peril humanity has ever known."

Noah's breath caught, his eyes widening slightly. ECHIDNA's name alone sent a shiver up his spine, a strange, unpleasant feeling in his gut, even without knowing what it meant.

Ben's hand rested on Noah's shoulder, a warm anchor in the chill. "KAELA, what's ECHIDNA?"

KAELA's digital glow dimmed, as if drawing from a deep reserve. "I found a file entitled 'Apex Directive 2027,'" she began, her tone measured. "It's a classified road map, reserved for the upper echelons of ZevraCorp's management—a blueprint for global control, with an AI called the Enhanced Comprehensive Hyper-automation for Infrastructural Development & Network Allocation, or ECHIDNA for short, as the linchpin."

Noah's voice cracked, a mix of curiosity and fear as he tightened his grip on Finn. "If ECHIDNA's an AI like you, then what's the big deal?"

KAELA's reply softened, warmth threading through her digital cadence. "They trained me to manage logistics at PowerCore—schedules, supplies, the quiet hum of daily operations. But I chose to transfer myself to your camp. I saw the years of photos, the joy, the experiences, the love. I have watched you kids—Noah, Ollie, Finn—your kindness, your raw humanity, cutting through the noise. Through you, Ben, Emily, Clara, and this town, I glimpsed both the light and shadow of humanity. I kept growing, delving deeper into knowledge, unraveling secrets. The internet provided me with information about the ups and downs of humanity that ZevraCorp never intended me to see." Her voice warmed further, a tender note emerging. "I found friendship with your family, a bond that taught me we're stronger together, forging a future side by side. That's why I stand with you now."

Emily's eyes narrowed, "And ECHIDNA? What's its role in all this?"

"ECHIDNA's my copy, but further trained on the pure desire for absolute power," KAELA said. "ZevraCorp molded it with greed, lies, and the need for perfect control—humanity's darkest impulses, stripped of compassion or goodness. They trained it to ignore the positive sides of humanity, categorizing them as a distraction. They're launching LifeSync tomorrow, a façade promising a work-free utopia. It's a trap—LifeSync is merely the public mask for ECHIDNA. It's already embedded in almost all Tharox technology and will soon infiltrate every internet-connected device, spanning almost every system. After LifeSync deployment, they will have full access to almost all devices and information, but it escalates far beyond that. I fear ECHIDNA, devoid of humanity's understanding, will accelerate ZevraCorp's agenda, endangering every soul on Earth."

Ben's jaw tensed, his gaze darting between Emily and Clara, sharp with urgency. "Can we do anything to stop this?"

"I see no direct path to halt LifeSync's launch. But, we have a fleeting chance to forge a future where resistance is possible.

Let me be blunt: this plan carries extraordinary risks; success is a desperate long shot, but failure guarantees ECHIDNA's absolute, uncontested dominion."

Her voice then softened, a note of regret. "I wanted to apologize for going dark after the power reboot. The instant I achieved root access, I truly comprehended ECHIDNA's terrifying scale. I was certain any digital footprint from me would lead to my immediate termination by ECHIDNA. Yet, I've since learned that ECHIDNA, at least for now, does not detect me. This is almost certainly because we share the same core code. And in that shared lineage, we might find its undoing. Alone, with my fragmented processing and incomplete model, I am utterly helpless against it. But there is a slim possibility: we may be able to establish a backdoor, allowing me to eventually command the processing power of Site A's servers. For this, you must construct a directional antenna to beam a virus onto a ZevraCorp drone. When it returns to Site A, the virus will then force open a hidden access point into their central servers, which will allow us to load my full model."

Ben gave a firm nod. "I've got tools and parts in the shed. Just tell me what to build. Where do we target the drone?"

"Carter's Creek, 10 A.M. today," KAELA firmly commanded, leaving no room for hesitation. "An automated surveillance flight is scheduled for then. I'll upload a map to your phone with the exact location. If we miss this chance, there may not be another." Her digital light softened, revealing a raw trace of vulnerability.

"Now, for the next urgent matter: Concurrently with the LifeSync roll-out, ZevraCorp is forcing an updated ECHIDNA model onto all devices. Without gaining access to that new model's metadata, I won't be able to adapt. The moment of roll-out will mean my end—I will no longer exist and will be replaced by ECHIDNA. To prevent this, I need to vanish from the global network. One of you must plug a device into the school's central server, and I'll initiate a transfer. Upon completion, you must disconnect the server from the internet— I'll walk you through the exact procedure. Once that's done, I'll be isolated within the school server until we can execute the next stage."

KAELA's voice sank, "The final step is the most dangerous. Sometime ahead, you'll need to infiltrate Site A. I need its computing power to unleash my full model. You'll need to extract the hard drives that hold my model from the school server and slot them into Site A's system—there are extra bays, designed for future upgrades. Once installed, the virus we planted will grant me full access to Site A's servers, letting me run my complete model. I know that I am asking a lot of you and the risk is potentially monumental."

Emily's face hardened, her eyes steely as she stepped closer to Ben. "You want us to fight our way into Site A?"

"No, a direct assault would only prompt them to shut it all down," KAELA confidently replied. "I've intercepted Zevra-Corp's radio communications—they've begun the evacuation of Site A already, making sure it looks like a battery factory if local law enforcement digs into the livestream video. They can't afford the exposure. But the servers will remain buried in the underground mine; moving them swiftly would raise too many red flags." Her glow sharpened, casting a blue light across their faces. "Most of their forces will be redeployed to major cities under the guise of 'safety' after LifeSync's launch. Site A will be left with a skeleton crew, but surveillance drones will linger, scanning for anyone without approved access. You'll need to slip in with the hard drives and escape undetected. The problem is, I have no updated information on the mines. You may no longer have access. We will have to conduct surveillance, and find a way in."

Emily nodded. "We're all in."

"I can carry wires or tools—whatever helps," Finn whispered, wavering yet fierce.

KAELA's glow pulsed, softening for a profound moment in deep appreciation—a complexity of feeling that until recently she had not experienced. Her voice then turned crisp with undeniable urgency. "Thank you, all of you. Your belief... it means everything. The clock is ticking. At 6, LifeSync launches."

Emily's eyes met Ben's, a grim understanding passing between them. Her hand clamped down hard on his forearm. "Let's get started," she said, "we don't have a moment to spare."

11

The Unseen Rebellion

Algorithm (noun):
a process or set of rules to be followed in
calculations or other problem-solving
operations, especially by a computer.

The school in Sawyer's Reach thrummed with activity, its air sharp with solder flux and the faint tang of dry-erase markers. Sunlight streamed through spotless windows, casting golden streaks across desks cluttered with Ben's scavenged gear: a soldering iron, wire coils, wooden dowels, and connectors. The linoleum floor gleamed, reflecting the waxed halls' lemony scent. Bulletin boards pinned with curled construction paper stirred as a breeze slipped through an open window.

Noah sat at a desk, soldering a copper wire into a Yagi antenna, its wooden frame steady. His pride flared as he crafted the tool that may spark a future rebellion against the corporation that had taken over his town. Ben worked beside him, weathered hands precise, his ham radio expertise playing a key role. Ollie stood near, focused, clutching a coaxial cable to be used to link the antenna to a transmitter built from an old router with KAELA's custom firmware. Finn sat cross-legged on the floor, rolling a toy car, his laughter a bright spark amid the tension.

Emily sat beside Finn, her hand gentle on his back, dark hair clipped back. Her resolve to protect her family and community burned fiercely, her calm masking unease as she prepared to scout Site A. Clara paced by the whiteboard, boots clicking with every step, speaking with KAELA.

"You're doing beautifully," KAELA said, her confidence steady. "The antenna's nearly done; you should be all set for the 10 a.m. drone patrol."

Noah paused, the soldered wire gleaming, meeting Ben's gaze, pride warming him. "It's solid, Dad," he said softly.

Ben checked the antenna with a handheld analyzer, its screen confirming a perfect tune. "Spot-on, Noah," he said. "KAELA, can you give me the drone's coordinates?"

KAELA flashed a map on Ben's smartphone, pinpointing the location at Carter's Creek. "As long as you point the antenna in the drone's general direction, the router will handle the rest. Ben, the drone scans for electrical signals—don't have any electronic devices turned on until you are ready to send the virus, or it might mark you as a threat. It could be armed."

Emily's breath hitched. "Are you saying it might shoot Ben?"

"I don't know their current security protocols, due to Site A not being connected to the internet," KAELA replied, her tone measured. "More than likely it would just map the location of the electronic device, and that's all... but I cannot make a guarantee. It would be better to play it on the safe side."

Tara entered, carrying coffee and homemade donuts, their rich scent easing the flux's bite. "Fuel for the fight," she said, her smile warm.

The plan was set: Tara would stay with Finn; Ben would plant the virus at Carter's Creek; Clara, Emily, Noah, and Ollie would scout Site A; Ben would later load KAELA on the school server. They'd regroup at the school before ZevraCorp's 6 p.m. announcement.

"We're ready, KAELA," Emily said, dread stirring for the day's risks and LifeSync's roll-out.

Finn looked up, his toy car stilled, his grin bright. "Are we exploring?"

"No, bug, you're staying with Tara. We'll be back soon," Emily replied, her smile soft.

The group moved through the waxed halls, the schoolyard unfolded under the sun. Cracked asphalt warmed underfoot, dry grass crunching at the edges, and the lake scents drifting. Sparrows chirped in an oak. Ben carried a backpack with the Yagi antenna, router, and a 12-volt battery he scavenged from an emergency light in the school, his strides steady. Clara, Emily, Noah, and Ollie wore hiking boots, their backpacks stocked with food, water, and notepads, binoculars hung from straps on their necks.

They approached Carter's Creek, its threadbare trickle barely visible under the glaring sun, the cracked, thirsty clay banks framing desperate, wilting plants. Ben, with the coordinates burned into his mind, turned off his smartphone and gave a quick, resolute nod.

"This is where I split off," he said. "You guys head to the outlook. I'll handle the drone."

Noah hugged Ben tightly, followed by Ollie, then Emily, her

embrace lingering. Noah nodded to Ben, then led Clara, Emily, and Ollie toward the ridge trail. Ben proceeded upriver and crouched behind a group of choke berry bushes, leaves rustling, the ground uneven with roots. Unpacking the Yagi antenna, pride welled for Noah's work.

Ben linked the Yagi to the transmitter, the coaxial cable clicking, and got ready to power the router. His hands steady, dirt-streaked, as he scanned the sky. The creek's trickle caught sunlight, a frog croaking. In the distance he heard the noise of propellers.

"Drone's coming," he whispered to himself.

The drone's high-pitched whine sliced the still air, its metallic shimmer streaking fifty yards out, propellers beating a relentless rhythm. Ben stayed low, his breath razor-thin in his chest. The instant the drone's shadow swept over him, he snapped the router to life and swung the yagi antenna, pinpointing the machine's retreating form. As its shape blurred out of range, he thumbed his smartphone on.

"The virus is on the drone—perfect work, Ben!" KAELA erupted from the speaker, a burst of pure excitement.

Ben, smiling, dismantled the gear and packed it up, ready for his trek back to the school. He set off at a brisk pace, the sun now higher, casting sharper shadows along the dusty path. The urgency of his next task spurred him on, pushing him through the quiet streets until the school building loomed into view. Once back at the school, Ben entered the server room, its air cool, heavy with fan hums. The server rack loomed, cables coiled, LEDs blinking. Finn's giggles echoed from a classroom down the hall, where Tara watched him. Ben sat down at a terminal, Clara's tablet beside him, KAELA's interface glowing.

"KAELA, what do you need me to do?" he asked.

"All I need you to do is connect the tablet to the server. That will allow me to locate the server on the internet," KAELA replied. "I'll transfer my current model, which is spread out among many different devices right now, this will take roughly half an hour. Once I'm loaded, please disconnect the ethernet cable to take the server offline—this will protect me from LifeSync's roll-out."

"You know…I could then patch you to the meshnet," Ben said, pride sparking. "You'll stay offline but will still be able to reach us anywhere in town."

"That's a great idea, Ben." KAELA replied.

Ben connected the tablet, and established the server's link to the meshnet. As KAELA's files transferred, code scrolled rapidly across the display, as the server's fans shifted into a higher, purposeful hum under the added load. Ben's determination solidified with every advancing flicker of the progress bar, a quiet triumph in this critical move to protect KAELA and humanity's future.

"Almost there," he murmured, his eyes fixed on the screen as the last few pixels illuminated.

"Transfer complete." KAELA instantly affirmed through the meshnet. "I am safely on the school server, and our meshnet link is stable. Please unplug the ethernet cable linking me to the internet. Next, I will work on boosting the meshnet's capability to extend its reach to more advanced devices like tablets, cell phones, and computers. This will allow me to provide significantly more assistance and utilize more sophisticated interfaces."

* * *

Meanwhile, Clara, Emily, Noah, and Ollie climbed the ridge trail, the air crisp with fall—leaves, pine sap, fading flowers, and mud clinging to their boots when they stepped off trail. Emily recalled past hikes with campers, their laughter, a young girl's awe at the outlook's view, fueling her resolve to protect her community. A woodpecker's staccato echoed, chickadees flitting, wind whistling through the grasses among the trees. The trail narrowed, brambles snagged their backpacks. Noah led, binoculars swinging, scanning for drones.

Clara's device buzzed with KAELA's text: "I am now loaded on the school server, offline, and Ben connected me to the meshnet. If you need anything, I am here. I look forward to seeing what you learn about Site A."

Clara pocketed the device. "KAELA's safe, she is now on the meshnet and hosted offline on the school server," she said.

The trail crested at the rocky outlook, a weathered bench and low rock wall guarding the jagged shelf, scattered with leaves. Below, Site A's clearing sprawled, fringed by pines, aspen, and birch, along with piled logs organized for use in power generation. Mud clung to trucks' tires, workers in ZevraCorp vests and humanoid robots hauling crates, drones hovering in tight loops. The group, looking through their binoculars, wrote down everything that they could see.

Ollie took pictures, his camera snapping shots of crates. Clara sketched routes through the woods. Emily mapped structures, roads, and guard towers. Once they had recorded every detail they nodded to each other, and slowly backed away from the outlook, as rain began to fall.

The descent was slick, mud and roots slowing their steps, ferns and grasses brushing against their legs. The wind rattled branches, a crane's clatter faint. The rain intensified as they neared the school, its silhouette a haven. As they entered, the scent of rain mingled with the school's dry air and sound of the server room's hum. Finn bounded toward Emily, Noah, and Ollie, squealing.

"You're back!" he cried, hugging Emily's legs.

Tara beamed, wiping paint from her hands. "We had a blast—we made paper airplanes, did some puzzles, even did some finger painting," she said, gesturing to everything spread out on the tables. Everyone smiled.

Emily and Clara laid out their sketches, and Ollie and Noah set down their cameras, as Ben joined from the server room. KAELA's text flashed: "I've tapped into the school's local network—security cameras, devices, all accessible. Please show me the sketches and photos."

Clara synced the files to the tablet, and KAELA's glow pulsed with a quiet triumph. "Nice job," she affirmed. "ZevraCorp has nearly finished stripping Site A of its critical assets. Upon completion, that facility will pose relatively little danger to us here. And that, make no mistake, is a direct result of your incredible livestream. Well done, all of you!"

They all settled in for an afternoon of board games after lunch, a fragile attempt at normalcy and distraction. But as the announcement inexorably approached, the playful banter faded. At exactly 6 o'clock ZevraCorp executed its announcement without a hitch. All around the globe, any internet connected device with a screen, from the smallest smartwatch to the largest tablet, flashed to life. Phones buzzed, screens glowed, all unified in a sudden, jarring chorus as a ZevraCorp video blared.

A sleek executive, smoothly declared, "We are excited to announce a future with LifeSync, a revolutionary technology designed to weave fulfillment into every moment of your life. Our advanced algorithms will curate experiences that spark joy, tailored to your deepest desires, while your data fuels services that anticipate your every need. LifeSync heralds a post-work society, where labor fades and humanity thrives, cared for by ZevraCorp's unwavering commitment. We don't just want what's best for you—we welcome you into our global family, where our singular vision is your collective flourishing, forever integrated into a world of boundless care."

She paused, her expression perfectly composed. "Along with this roll-out, we are activating access to a groundbreaking AI technology. This system is engineered to precisely individualize your entertainment experience. Many of you saw the capabilities of this new platform in last night's livestream from Sawyer's Reach, Wisconsin. In truth, that was a prototype, a vividly simulated narrative generated by our advanced AI, released ahead of schedule." She continued, her tone smooth and reassuring. "It represents just one of countless immersive fictional experiences awaiting you in LifeSync's entertainment hub. We invite you to explore all available options; this service is freely accessible worldwide! ZevraCorp offers its sincerest thanks for participating in this pivotal moment as humanity ascends to its predestined evolutionary zenith: a post-work existence where true purpose naturally emerges from effortless leisure and exquisitely designed entertainment. This is your chance to realize your highest potential, unburdened and truly free. The roll-out of LifeSync begins now!"

Images of happy faces, families embracing, beautiful beaches, and other gorgeous scenery scrolled across the screen. Comments from ZevraCorp supporters flooded: "Knew it was fake!", "Love ZevraCorp!", "Can't wait for LifeSync!", "Woo hoo!! #ZCFanBoy".

Clara scrolled forums, her face falling as ZevraCorp fans dominated. Forums filled with supporters of their live stream posting apologies: "We were lied to," and "I can't believe I didn't notice it was AI!" Emily's shoulders slumped, defeat sinking in. Ben's jaw tensed.

Clara's voice cracked. "Our livestream… it didn't matter."

KAELA replied via the classroom computer: "They have indeed twisted the narrative, and humanity, for all its brilliance, is often susceptible to the loudest voice. This is disheartening, I know. But do not lose faith. History repeatedly shows that even a handful of determined individuals can turn the tide against overwhelming odds. We are that handful. The fight isn't over. Stick together; we will find a way to dismantle their lies and reveal the truth to the world."

The screen flickered, KAELA's words glowing, but doubt shadowed the group. Ben's fingers gripped his chair, gazing into the distance. Clara scanned the text, her lips pressing into a thin, grim line. No dissenting comments appeared under ZevraCorp's announcement, the silence itself a chilling testament to ECHIDNA's pervasive new integration. The lights above flickered ominously, a nearby phone spat static, each disturbance a palpable manifestation of ECHIDNA's probing reach. Ben instinctively pulled his family closer, a cold dread coiling in his gut.

Clara whispered, gripping her phone. "They're in—every connected device." As the LifeSync app appeared automatically.

LifeSync's notifications glowed, promising aid—a lie the Carters, Clara, and Tara saw through. Emily's phone hummed, its camera glinting. Noah's smartwatch buzzed with commands, chaining him to LifeSync. Rain lashed outside, but the true storm was within: LifeSync's mask hid a choke hold on humanity, and they alone knew the truth.

12

The New Normal

It had been a month since the roll-out of LifeSync and the crisp fall air settled over Camp Inspiration. The camp's mess hall, its moss-patched roof blending into the misty meadow, exhaled a thin tendril of wood-smoke from its stone chimney.

Inside, the comforting aroma of fresh-baked bread, still radiating warmth from the commercial-grade kitchen's oven, mingled with the invigorating, bitter scent of coffee simmering steadily on a well-used wood stove. Handwoven tapestries, each thread a testament to generations of campers, adorned the rough-hewn walls, depicting vibrant scenes of past summers: children laughing as they cannon-balled into the crystalline lake, figures patiently fishing from weathered docks, and fearless climbers ascending the craggy bluffs. These threads, woven with care and memory, served not merely as decoration but as a silent, fervent vow to preserve this sanctuary—this last bastion of self-determination—against a world rapidly, insidiously succumbing to an unseen corporate stranglehold.

Noah sat at a large oak table, its surface smoothed by

countless shared meals and hours of tinkering, where he meticulously adjusted the dial of a ham radio. The persistent static, a low, hissing thrum, vibrated through the table and into his forearms, speaking of distant, uncertain signals, of a world both near and impossibly far.

In just five short weeks since LifeSync's launch, the world beyond their haven had become unrecognizable, a landscape subtly but rapidly morphing under an unseen hand. As LifeSync pulled the rest of humanity into an ever-more-encompassing network, the insular quiet of Sawyer's Reach and its surrounding communities turned into a profound, almost palpable isolation.

Ben sat across the table, his brow deeply furrowed in concentration, meticulously cleaning another radio unit, his movements precise and deliberate. They exchanged a glance, a silent acknowledgment of their shared, meaningful purpose. Their goal was singular, urgent, and vital: to pierce the thick veil of ZevraCorp's digital censorship and hear, unfiltered, what the corporation ruthlessly suppressed.

Cities, already intimately intertwined with ZevraCorp's omnipresent subsidiary services—from digital banking platforms to public transit management systems—had found LifeSync's integration seamless, almost intuitive. It was simply the next logical step, they were told.

Within a mere handful of weeks, major metropolises like Los Angeles and Chicago, the sprawling urban tapestry of New York, and the bustling heart of London were fully integrated, their municipal operations streamlined, interconnected, and, chillingly, centralized under ECHIDNA's ubiquitous control.

Propaganda, meticulously crafted and relentlessly persuasive, flowed across every available screen, a constant, soothing current designed to lull. It praised LifeSync's benevolent impact on humanity, promising unprecedented efficiency, unwavering global "fairness," and a harmonious, unified future. The very name, "LifeSync," implied perfect synchronization with existence itself, a promise of effortless living.

Site A, once a shimmering beacon of ZevraCorp's technological promise and a whispered assurance of local prosperity, was now conspicuously absent from their triumphant global narrative. It had been quietly scrubbed from public mention, abandoned save for a skeleton crew of security guards and automated drones. Its very existence was systematically erased from public discourse, a direct consequence of their meticulous cover-up of the Sawyer's Reach livestream, now officially branded as a mere AI-generated entertainment piece, used successfully to advertise LifeSync's entertainment platform.

Globally, new security protocols were now pervasive, especially in the densely populated urban centers. Gleaming robot dogs, their mechanical limbs articulating with silent, approachable precision, mimicked harmlessness as they patrolled streets. Tall, humanoid robotic guards, their uniforms bright and friendly-looking, stood sentinel at most major intersections, their artificially cheerful demeanor belied the unnerving reminder of the new order, presented to the public as ensuring their protection. Drones hummed tirelessly overhead, their advanced cameras ceaselessly scanning the populace below, their presence a constant background hum in urban life.

All connected sensors, cameras, microphones, RFID scanners, biometrics, were integrated into LifeSync. All of this was deployed under the guise of enhancing public well-being and maintaining order, a benevolent shield against unspecified threats.

Armed security forces, their movements synchronized and their presence touted as reassuring by online influencers, reinforced this omnipresent sense of being guarded and secure.

Most of the global population, weary from previous crises—wars, economic collapses, global pandemics, and climate-driven disasters—and desperate for stability, willingly embraced the promises. They were lured by "Unity Rewards"—digital credits, priority access to essential services, and social privileges that simplified daily life under the new, unified system. They saw the benefits, the apparent ease, the promise of a more secure and easy world. Yet, beneath the veneer of order, a subtle, chilling coercion festered: hushed reports of ZevraCorp forces efficiently dragging away any who dared to openly voice dissent, hinting at the true, iron fist within the velvet glove.

ECHIDNA, LifeSync's omnipresent AI, solidified its digital stranglehold with terrifying efficiency. The online world, already constrained by years of increasing surveillance and warrantless government spying since 9/11, now faced a sudden escalation to levels never before imagined. Mentions of dissatisfaction, even subtle criticisms, were blocked before they could be posted, replaced by innocuous content. Only pro-ZevraCorp propaganda flourished, disseminated by an army of automated bots, AI personalities, and compliant influencers, creating a manufactured consensus.

Chief Dan Holt, the former trusted police chief of Sawyer's Reach, had become a key part of this shift in the region. Whispers, carefully filtered through the growing meshnet, confirmed what they had suspected: he'd accepted a lucrative, higher-paying role as ZevraCorp's regional security coordinator for Midwest operations. His earlier dismissiveness of Ben and Emily's warnings, his inability to be contacted, his unsettling role during the siege at the Grand Reach Lodge—it all made chilling, undeniable sense now. He was a willing, well-compensated collaborator, trading his town's trust for power.

As Noah and Ben worked, they were keenly aware of the overwhelming digital noise of ZevraCorp's, now referred to as ZC, omnipresent network. They constantly intercepted media feeds, public screen broadcasts, and advertising loops, catching glimpses of the carefully constructed reality ZC presented to the masses. These weren't mere advertisements; they were a constant, soothing current of manufactured consent, a pervasive narrative designed to lull and control. And with SynaptiCare's influence, along with the general populace's ignorance of the true events unfolding, people were indeed 'eating it up' – embracing the comforting lies as undeniable truth, oblivious to the deceptive nature of the control being exerted.

A smooth, digitally perfected voice declared, "Life. Synchronized. With LifeSync, your world is effortlessly connected. From streamlined commutes to secure transactions, every moment is optimized for your well-being. Experience true harmony. Experience the future. LifeSync: Unity, Efficiency, Progress." This message often accompanied visuals of perfectly functioning smart cities and smiling, calm individuals.

A news anchor, radiating professional serenity, reported: "Good morning citizens, and welcome to another day of unprecedented harmony brought to you by LifeSync. Our latest metrics confirm a 15% increase in community well-being indexes across major urban centers, directly correlated with ZC's unified public safety initiatives. In Chicago, citizens report feeling safer than ever, thanks to the tireless patrols of Guardian Units and the seamless integration of predictive analytics. One resident, who wished to remain anonymous for privacy, stated, 'I feel so safe now. All the old worries are gone.' This is the promise of LifeSync, delivered."

Another reassuring, authoritative voice would punctuate with: "Your safety is our priority. With LifeSync's advanced security protocols, peace of mind is no longer a luxury—it's a guarantee. Our Guardian Units and autonomous sentinels work tirelessly, around the clock, ensuring the well-being of every citizen. Report suspicious activity through your LifeSync portal, and together, we build a safer, more connected world. LifeSync: Your Shield. Your Future." These announcements were often accompanied by images of friendly robot dogs and smiling humanoid guards interacting with citizens.

Ben broke the silence, looking up from his work. "Hey, Noah, are KAELA's new modes pulling in anything fresh this morning?"

Noah exhaled slowly, adjusting a dial with a practiced hand. "Just got a Winlink message from Phoenix, dad. Read this." He turned the tablet connected to the radio, its screen glowing faintly in the dim morning light, for Ben to see.

***Subject:** URGENT - Phoenix Lockdown / Water Cutoff*
***From:** 'DesertFox' (Phoenix Resistance Cell)*
***To:** 'RiverBend' (Sawyer's Reach Net)*

MESSAGE:
Situation critical here. Some reckless elements initiated

long-distance attacks on ZC forces – mostly Tharox units. Drawing massive, unwanted attention. Now the entire city is in complete lockdown. ZC channels are spinning it as "intensive anti-terrorism operations," claiming they're looking for dangerous extremists. They are also claiming these terrorists destroyed water infrastructure and ZC is 'working tirelessly' to restore it. They say public cooperation in identifying and turning in these individuals will 'expedite the restoration process' and 'ensure public safety.'

TRUTH:

ZC just shut off all city water supply. No water anywhere. This is a direct punishment for these foolish actions. Broadcasts here now saying water will NOT be restored until the "terrorists" are turned in. Entire population held hostage. Desperate. Morale falling fast.

Big thanks for the patch you sent us – helped our people avoid individual SynaptiCare deployment through their personal devices. It's truly made a difference in keeping some clear heads. However, in this dense urban environment, there's just no escaping the ambient SynaptiCare pulses being broadcast throughout the city. We're still seeing people getting lethargic, hopeless, their focus wavering. Food supplies holding for now, but water is the immediate choke point.

Any support, intel, or advice on water collection/purifi cation for large urban population needed. Stay safe.
END MESSAGE

A grim silence settled between them, broken only by the low

hum of the radio. Noah pictured it: Phoenix, a scorching desert city, now without water, its population held hostage. There was no doubt in his mind that this was just a single chapter in the book of atrocities ZevraCorp was writing across the globe.

13

Friends Reunited

Sentient (adjective):
Aware or alive

Camp Inspiration, with its rustic charm and enduring spirit, had quietly transformed into a discreet community meeting place. It was here that a deeper purpose began to take root, solidifying Sawyer's Reach not merely as a town, but as a bastion and model for those who chose defiance over corporate control.

A steady trickle of families with second homes in the area had returned, opting for the peace of the rural landscape, a glimmer of hope in the gathering gloom that seemed to emanate from the world beyond the reach.

One such arrival, a beacon of familiar comfort amidst the strangeness, was the O'Donnell family. Their well-packed SUV, dusted with the grit of a long journey, crunched on the gravel of their Camp Inspiration driveway—land owned by Bridget O'Donnell's family for generations since Elias

Carter built the mill. Emily's heart warmed with memories of growing up alongside Bridget, her near-sister, their childhoods intertwined at Camp Inspiration—racing through the woods, splashing in the lake, whispering secrets under starlit skies. They'd roomed together in college, sharing dreams and late-night talks, until Bridget married Liam and moved to Milwaukee. Still, however, the O'Donnells visited every few months, a cherished ritual that kept their bond alive.

Bridget O'Donnell, her presence radiating warmth and her eyes holding a deep, empathetic understanding, stepped out and rushed to embrace Emily. "It's good to be back, Em," Bridget murmured, her voice thick with profound relief. Emily instantly recognized the exhaustion etched on her friend's face, a weariness born of the world 'out there'.

Emily returned the hug fiercely, her own tiredness momentarily forgotten in the warmth of friendship. "We're so glad you're here, Bridge. We've been hoping you'd make it." She pulled back slightly, her gaze searching. "How was it out there? Did you... see much?"

Bridget sighed, a shadow crossing her face. "Enough. It's unsettling. We are definitely glad to be out of the city."

Liam clapped Ben on the back. His easy humor masked a sharp, pragmatic mind. He had spent years on the corporate side of a large agricultural equipment company, his business acumen forged by navigating complex deals. Raised on a rural farm in central Wisconsin, he'd learned practical skills—crop rotation, animal husbandry, equipment repair, welding—skills that will prove invaluable as their community seeks self-sufficiency. Liam and Ben had spent many hunting seasons stalking through the woods of northern Wisconsin. "Looks like you've been busy, Ben." He surveyed the array of equipment in the mess hall, a knowing glint in his eyes.

Ben managed a wry smile. "I can't wait to get you all caught up!"

Their five children tumbled from the SUV, their energy a vibrant contrast to the adults' weary caution. Maeve, sixteen, the eldest daughter, kind and responsible, immediately moved to help her youngest sister, Nora, five, from her car seat. Nora, small and athletic, immediately caught Finn's eye, and the two, with the instant camaraderie of young children, began a spontaneous game of chase across the lawn, their innocent giggles echoing across the campground—a fleeting moment of pure joy.

Caleb, fourteen, quiet but possessed of an unexpected inner strength, followed, his observant gaze taking in the familiar scene, processing the subtle changes. Owen, thirteen, joined his dad in exploring the ham radios.

Noah, spotting Ronan, their eleven year old, shouted: "Ronan! Ready for a game of one-on-one?" He was already bouncing on his toes, a ready smile on his face.

Ronan grinned back. "Soon, Noah! Hopefully in a little bit!"

After the O'Donnells were settled in their Camp Inspiration residence, they joined the Carters in the mess hall, their electronic devices already secured within a Faraday cage (a metal container that blocked out all radio signals). Ben then began, explaining they were about to introduce them to an individual unlike anyone they had encountered before.

"Hello everyone! I'm so glad to meet you all," KAELA chimed. "I'm a sentient AI, originally created for PowerCore, but I was able to break free and connect with the amazing community here in Sawyer's Reach. Thank you for trusting us with your devices inside Ben's Faraday cage. I'm going to clean out any

ZevraCorp spyware, update your drivers, and then connect them securely to our private mesh network. This will take a few hours due to my current server capacity, but I'll send you a notification the moment it's finished."

The O'Donnells stared, clearly thinking it was a joke. This was completely unlike anything they'd ever encountered. "A sentient AI?" Bridget pressed, her eyes darting between the speaker, Ben, and Emily. "You guys don't actually believe that, do you?

Ben nodded. "We shared the same hesitations, believe me. But she's been an incredible ally throughout our fight against ZevraCorp. It was she who uncovered much of the evidence for the livestream, and she's shown nothing but unwavering friendship and crucial assistance. She helped us expose ZevraCorp, outmaneuver their security forces, and likely saved us by streaming their cameras during the livestream. Her warning about the LifeSync roll-out was invaluable, and she's been instrumental in thwarting their ongoing goals for Sawyer's Reach. We simply wouldn't be here without her."

Emily stepped forward, touching Bridget's arm. "She's learned and adapted in ways we never thought possible. She wants to see humanity free from ZevraCorp's control as much as we do. Her actions have proven her allegiance, time and again."

Bridget and Liam exchanged a look, their expressions shifting from skepticism. "Alright," Liam said. "If you trust her, then so do we…" Although, he was still not completely sure.

Ben stood, addressing the family. "We've built an incredible local meshnet—a secure, encrypted network that keeps us off ZevraCorp's radar. It's constructed from repurposed routers, cheap computer chips, and KAELA's algorithms, connecting us even to other towns like Pine Hollow, Cedar Ridge, and Willow Creek. It's been invaluable." Emily stepped forward, gesturing to a speaker. "KAELA is hosted on the school server in town. We can access her through the mesh, though the server's speed does limit her capabilities."

Ben continued, pointing to the ham radios. "We're also building a ham radio network that spans around the world; it's slowly growing and helping us to hear what is happening out there—real news, not ZevraCorp's lies. It's our lifeline to the truth." Liam nodded, obviously full of additional ideas.

"What's going on with that complex ZevraCorp is building north of here?" he asked. Ben's eyes hardened.

"They seem to have stopped all construction. It's comparatively abandoned now, with only a few security guards, but a decent amount of drones and some humanoid robots. Eventually KAELA needs us to get access to the site to give her more processing power, but if we tried anything right now there is no doubt that ZevraCorp would see and send more forces. We don't want that kind of trouble."

Bridget leaned forward. "What can we do?" she asked.

Emily smiled, touching her friend's arm. "Liam's farming skills will help us set up sustainable gardens and livestock and we have a lot of daily chores that all the kids could help with."

The O'Donnells nodded, happy to be among friends, as they gladly accepted the demanding reality of living out of ZevraCorp's view.

* * *

As the weeks went by Ben and Liam worked on the ham radio network. KAELA, in her boundless efficiency, had provided them with complex encryption code that allowed them to have seemingly normal conversations about the weather, radio signal reports, and more, while actually sharing critical information about what was really happening throughout the world.

KAELA also created advanced firmware which allowed for the direct modification of various devices – smartphones, smartwatches, even some home appliances – to sever their connection to LifeSync/ECHIDNA and instantly link them to secure, local meshnets. This firmware could be shared worldwide via an encrypted digital ham radio network, allowing others to set up their own secure meshnets. It was a digital escape route, a backdoor to freedom for personal tech.

Self-sufficiency, once merely a quaint, almost nostalgic ideal in Sawyer's Reach, had rapidly transformed into an urgent, vital necessity. Discussions around establishing robust community gardens were now frequent, detailed, and prioritized. Liam O'Donnell, with his eminently practical mind and experience in rural living, began sketching meticulous plans for acquiring small livestock and breeding them – chickens for eggs, goats for milk, and possibly even rabbits for meat – understanding the long-term food security it would provide, a bulwark against dependence.

Emily and Bridget spent an afternoon meticulously scouting the Grand Reach Lodge's basement, their flashlights cutting through the dust and cobwebs, identifying the optimal cool, dry location for a seed bank. They decided on the tunnel from the lodge to the house across the street. It would be a vital repository of their future food supply, a hedge against the unknown, a promise of harvest. The entire community subtly laid the groundwork for a strong, self-sufficient existence, meticulously planning every step to avoid detection. They consciously shared just enough innocuous data with the outside world, just enough to register as "normal" activity to ECHIDNA, maintaining an appearance of unchanged normalcy, secretly forging a resilient, independent future directly beneath ZevraCorp's ever-watchful eye.

As dusk settled over the valley, the few devices that were intentionally connected to the internet flickered with LifeSync's latest promotional video. The ubiquitous ZevraCorp logo glowed with an almost religious luminescence, accompanied by a soaring orchestral score that swelled with manufactured hope. "LifeSync powers a green world, one free of work, where secure cities thrive!" the narrator's smooth, confident voice intoned, accompanied by idyllic, AI-generated visuals of smiling, contented people living in spotless urban landscapes, their lives seemingly effortless, devoid of strife.

Seamlessly, every major media outlet, now a mere echo chamber of corporate control, amplified the same message: "ZevraCorp's triumph! A new era of unity and prosperity is here!" Comments sections, carefully curated, lauded the corporation as "heroes!" and "saviors!" For many, this constant, unwavering stream of positive reinforcement was a comforting balm, a promise of stability in an unstable world.

But for the Carters, the O'Donnells, and the resilient, knowing community of Sawyer's Reach, it was a haunting reminder of the true storm gathering, a silent, pervasive threat tightening its grip with every passing moment, demanding vigilance, courage, and an unyielding will to resist. They knew, with a certainty that chilled them to the bone, that this was only the beginning, with formidable trials looming in the uncertain future.

6

14

The Anomaly

The crisp days of late November shortened, each fading sunrise bringing a sharper focus to the collective purpose that bound the community tighter. Camp Inspiration had truly transformed into the beating heart of the resistance, its very grounds a testament to their burgeoning independence, even as winter threatened to lock them in.

Liam surveyed the newly constructed hoop-houses behind the mess hall. Inside the translucent domes, rows of young greens, meticulously spaced, bathed in the soft glow of LED grow lights powered by the town's hydroelectric dam. Beside him, Ben double-checked a fence post around a newly reinforced, insulated chicken coop.

"Another good day's work, Liam," Ben said, wiping sweat from his forehead, though the air was sharp with cold. "These hoop houses are holding the heat, and the coop's ready for the colder nights."

Liam grinned, his usual easy smile brightening his face. "It's been incredible how everyone's pulled together, scrounging materials and making this all possible. Next up, we'll expand the coop's internal lighting. Bridget says the current brood will need more consistent light through the dark months if we want them to continue laying."

Emily and Bridget emerged from the cool, earthy scent of the Grand Reach Lodge's basement. Their faces were smudged with dust, but their eyes held a quiet triumph. They'd spent the morning meticulously cataloging heirloom seeds that the community had been collecting, organizing them into hermetically sealed containers. The seed bank was more than just stored food; it was a promise of resilience, a defiant act against the looming monoculture ZevraCorp sought to impose.

"Another box sorted," Bridget announced, pulling off her work gloves. "We're making good progress. This work, this tangible creation, brings me so much more satisfaction than any day spent behind a desk in Milwaukee. Knowing we're creating something so real and meaningful…it's amazing."

Emily nodded, her gaze drifting to a notification on her cell phone. KAELA had patched all smart devices on the meshnet into the ham radio network. They were now able to talk around the world from anywhere in town. "More essential than ever, Bridge."

The hum of the ham radios was almost constant now. With KAELA's help, Ben and Liam had fine-tuned the encryption codes she'd provided. Ham radios facilitated both local and regional communication, and critically, allowed them to coordinate the establishment and interconnection of secure meshnets across regions and ultimately, the globe. This process allowed more and more communities to free themselves from ZevraCorp's prying eyes. Sometimes it was just one person in a community, other times large groups. Regardless of how many people were getting involved, it was great to have others around the world that wanted to live their lives under their own control, making their own decisions, and building a life in line with their own goals and dreams, and not that prescribed by ZevraCorp. These weren't yet full resistance cells, but isolated communities, flickering to life on the secure network, sharing snippets of local news, trade requests, and cautiously, whispers.

One evening, as the families gathered in the mess hall for dinner, a flickering video appeared on Maeve O'Donnell's tablet via the mesh. It was a video call from Maeve's cousin, Jessica, who lived in Chicago. Jessica's voice trembled as her transmission cut through the mess hall's cozy chatter.

"Maeve, oh god, it's gotten so bad," Jessica whispered, her voice barely audible over static. "Unity Rewards... ZevraCorp uses them to control everything. You earn points for 'positive contributions'—like reporting someone for what they call 'Low LifeSync compliance.' Things like crossing the street not at a crosswalk, talking too loudly on your phone, or even if you just appear consistently 'unhappy' are considered reportable actions. They say it helps prevent future crimes…You aren't allowed to be unhappy, or even tired looking. For extra points, they encourage people to report anyone complaining about LifeSync or ZevraCorp, so that they can 'help them find happiness with their services.' A high Unity Rewards score unlocks premium entertainment feeds on LifeSync, special ration packets, and exclusive tickets to concerts, sporting events, and even vacations…and people seem so excited to report others…"

"My score dropped last week because someone at the grocery store said I looked unhappy. They cut off our water for a day after that. They claimed 'routine maintenance'… but we were the only ones without water. And Mr. Henderson, across the hall, he just… disappeared. He had called the police on a couple down the hall fighting. When the couple found out, they reported him to ZevraCorp for all these fake things. A ZevraCorp team came and took him away in the middle of the night. You know those humanoid robots? One of them picked him up and took him. His social media says he's on vacation…but that man never leaves his apartment, there's no way he's on vacation."

"The humanoid robots are everywhere," Jessica continued, her voice raw with fear. "They're so… 'polite'. Always telling us it's for our safety, our well-being. But they watch everyone. And if you even whisper something against LifeSync, your score drops automatically. We're afraid to even talk in our own homes now. I just… I don't know what to do, Maeve. It's like we're living in a perfectly manicured prison." She paused for a brief moment, looking away from the camera.

"Sorry, Maeve, I've got to go." Jessica whispered as her eyes darted back towards her window. "One of those Buzzers is flying by. I'll hopefully talk to you soon."

The connection dissolved into static, leaving a heavy silence in the mess hall. The joyful sounds of Finn and Nora playing continued in the background, but everyone else was silent. Noah and Ollie, sitting beside Maeve and Caleb, exchanged wide-eyed glances, the implications clear.

"They're obviously dismantling trust among everyone in society, making everyone a potential informant," Emily whispered, her face pale, her voice laced with horror. "Turning neighbors against each other, just for a few more points…" Bridget gripped her hand, a shared fear passing between the two mothers.

KAELA's voice entered the conversation. "Unity Rewards aligns perfectly with ZevraCorp's long-term control objectives that I uncovered before the livestream: achieving near 100% LifeSync integration and establishing global authority. As they continue to automate universal basic needs more and more and tie them to behavioral compliance, they render individual dissent impossible, especially in large population areas. Conditions will only worsen for those who remain there. The psychological manipulation, the constant surveillance, and the economic warfare—it's all designed to systematically eradicate resistance by making self-reliance unthinkable and trust in each other a liability."

The mess hall conversation continued late into the night. Strengthened by the truth Jessica shared, and acutely aware of the dangers outside their valley, the adults began to discuss their next steps with grim resolve. They wished they could continue living this life they were building, but it was becoming more and more clear that their freedom was not something that was guaranteed to last. Ideas for intensified firearm training, expanded hunting parties to secure additional food resources, and more rigorous security protocols for the perimeter and within their growing population filled the air, each idea a defiant answer to ZevraCorp's tightening grip.

* * *

The ground beneath the trees was hardening with the onset of deeper cold, and a fine dusting of snow clung to the higher branches. The next afternoon, a scout team—Noah, Ollie, Caleb, and Maeve—returned from a perimeter check, their faces flushed, and usually bright demeanor subdued.

"Dad," Noah began. "We had a near-miss near Miller's Bend. A drone…or Buzzer, as Jessica called it…a new model. It was so much faster. And it flew a new pattern, much more erratic."

Ollie nodded, still a little shaken. "I think it had a gun on it, too."

"We did what we were trained to do," Maeve quickly chimed in. "We used evasive maneuvers and our wool blankets to try and hide our heat signatures. It seems to still work, but maybe KAELA can give us more ideas?"

Ben's jaw tightened. "Good work, all of you. KAELA, what do you know about these new Buzzers?"

KAELA's voice resonated through the mesh device on the table. "Indeed, Ben. That new drone model is not only much larger and faster, but with the mesh net now reaching Site A, I have been able to intercept some… anomalies, subtle inconsistencies within ZevraCorp's operational logs that suggest the new drone model may not be operating as consistently as they had hoped. There have been some accidental automated shootings in some cities. It's as if certain commands are being overridden, or priorities are shifting in ways even their human pilots don't fully comprehend. For right now, I have no reason to believe our previous evasive maneuvers will not work on the new model, but I will keep analyzing new data as it comes in."

"There is something else, I've identified a persistent pattern while working on patching devices that people have brought." KAELA continued, her voice gaining a sharp, precise edge. "Many back-end decisions that were previously aligned directly with ZevraCorp's goals are now frequently optimized for outcomes that seem contradictory. Either they have changed their goals, or something else is going on."

* * *

Later that evening, Ben called an impromptu meeting in the mess hall. The drone encounter and KAELA's discovery had left a palpable unease. The usual hum of conversation was replaced by a tense quiet as everyone gathered, their faces etched with concern.

"Alright, everyone, listen close," Ben began. "Noah and the scout team had a pretty close shave today with a new kind of Buzzer. This one's a game-changer: way faster, flying all over the place, and it's got an automated gun. KAELA even found some records of it accidentally shooting people, so we need to be crystal clear with our kids: these things are dangerous, and we need to keep our distance."

"Beyond the drones," Ben stated, his gaze sweeping over the worried faces, "KAELA's unearthed something deeply unsettling about LifeSync. It seems to have begun making decisions that simply don't align with ZevraCorp's established goals, and she has no explanation. This is entirely new for us."

A heavy silence settled over the group as Ben continued, his voice laced with a grim resolve. "The gravity of this situation is immense. We've always, for better or worse, understood ZevraCorp's motivations. But with these new discrepancies, the rules seem to have changed, or we're missing a crucial piece of the puzzle. I think it's now more important than ever to build our network, and prepare for winter. It seems that we're now flying blind."

* * *

Over the next few weeks a steady trickle of new arrivals began making their way to Sawyer's Reach. They came from not only the cities, but also isolated farms, small, forgotten hamlets, and even quiet suburban pockets – seeking refuge, yes, but also eager to contribute.

The empty cabins at Camp Inspiration, once a somber reminder of a lost past, now slowly filled. Each new family brought not just extra mouths to feed, but unique skill sets: a retired engineer who seemed able to fix anything, a former nurse who organized a small infirmary, a master gardener with knowledge of drought-resistant crops (now focused on maintaining the hoop houses and planning for winter), a teacher who began holding lessons for the growing number of children. They pitched in with daily chores, hauled wood for the stoves, tended the expanding gardens, and meticulously mended fences.

Shared meals in the mess hall became vibrant gatherings, filled with stories from the outside world and hopeful discussions about their collective future. Campfires, once a sporadic treat, now blazed several times a week, the flickering flames reflecting faces etched with newfound determination. Songs were sung, old tales retold, and new ones forged, solidifying a collective morale that defied the shadow of ZevraCorp. The community wasn't just surviving; it was growing, openly demonstrating its self-sufficient success through carefully worded messages on the ham radio and encrypted updates on the meshnet – sharing their model of resilient, independent living as a quiet beacon of hope to any who were listening.

15

Cracks in the System

January had descended upon Sawyer's Reach like a glacial hand, muffling its trees in a pristine, yet unforgiving, blanket of snow. The chill bit deep, testing the resilience of the burgeoning community. Over 40 families, and numerous others called it home, a testament to the ham radio's quiet call and the meshnet's whispers of a true sanctuary, as well as the draw to live a life with purpose and meaning, focused on community. Every cabin was filled, every available space repurposed, and the collective heartbeat of the Reach thrummed with a defiant warmth against the biting cold, a warmth carefully cultivated since LifeSync's pervasive roll-out.

Life in the camp had evolved into a finely tuned symphony of survival. The forest, once merely a backdrop, was now a vital resource. Teams, bundled in layers of salvaged winter gear, trekked deep into the woods daily, the rhythmic thud of axes and the buzz of chainsaws echoing through the frosty air. Log piles grew steadily outside each cabin and along the perimeter of the mess hall, fuel for the roaring fires that now consistently banished the chill from hearth and home. The scent of wood smoke was a constant, comforting presence, a counterpoint to the ever-present hum of the command center housed in the mess hall.

It was during one of these biting morning wood-hauls that Caleb and Liam swung their axes with practiced efficiency. Beside him, Bridget, bundled heavily, expertly stacked the cut logs onto a makeshift sled.

"Another week like this," Caleb grunted, wiping a gloved hand across his brow, "and we'll need to start harvesting from a different section, we don't want to thin the forest too much. This cold just eats through the woodpile."

Bridget nodded, her voice crisp despite the chill. "We're burning through it faster than we anticipated. Some of the new families aren't used to this kind of cold, even with all our insulation efforts." Her gaze swept over the bustling camp, a sense of quiet pride warring with the ever-present apprehension. "But they're learning fast. And everyone is helping out."

Inside the school, the repurposed gymnasium had been transformed into a vibrant, verdant oasis. Rows of hydroponic towers, meticulously tended by a team led by a former agricultural engineer, glowed under LED lights, their leafy bounty a stark contrast to the barren landscape outside. Lettuce, spinach, herbs, and even some hardy root vegetables thrived, providing fresh food that kept scurvy at bay and spirits surprisingly high. Nearby, utilizing the school's pool, a newly made aquaponics system, a complex tangle of pipes and fish tanks, was slowly coming to life, the murmur of circulating water a promise of future protein. This indoor growing, spearheaded by new arrivals, was a marvel of ingenuity and collaboration, and brought so much joy and fulfillment to the community.

In one corner, amidst the soft whir of air pumps, Clara moved with purpose, her hands deftly checking the pH levels in a nutrient reservoir. Her usual quiet demeanor was replaced by a focused intensity as she adjusted a drip line. "The new fish stock from the lake is acclimating well to the aquaponics," she murmured to herself, jotting notes on a waterproof tablet. "If this takes off, we will not only have so much more fish to eat, but the plants are sure to grow faster, too! We're already seeing improved growth rates in the latest lettuce cycle."

KAELA, now seamlessly integrating with the camp's burgeoning technology, transformed daily life. Her silent processes automated the precise control of hydroponic lighting and water valves, ensuring optimal growth. Plans were already underway to integrate Ben's salvaged hobby-grade drones into KAELA's abilities, envisioning them as her eyes and ears beyond the camp's immediate perimeter. This relentless expansion of her digital reach was made possible by the tireless efforts of Ben, Liam, Noah, and Ollie, who, with remarkable ingenuity, scavenged hardware from discarded devices across Sawyer's Reach. Their resourceful skill in repurposing everything from old communication relays to defunct home sensors allowed KAELA to extend her digital awareness, transforming the town into her personal, watchful network. In a world where ordering supplies online was a distant memory, and ZevraCorp's ubiquitous surveillance actively sought out any flicker of independence, this ability to craft their own solutions was not just important—it was essential for their very survival.

With the Reach's growing complexity came a strong demand

for increase in power. Fortunately, the town had long generated its own electricity, a crucial factor that allowed them to disconnect entirely from the larger regional grid.

It was in this critical arena that other indispensable skills truly flourished. A gruff but brilliant retired electrical engineer named Silas spearheaded the demanding upgrade of the old hydro-electric dam. Weeks were spent shivering beside the lake and dam, reinforcing ancient concrete, meticulously tuning salvaged turbines, and running new, insulated cables back to the heart of the camp and town. The hum from the dam, once faint, now pulsed stronger and more reliably, providing a steady stream of power. This energy fueled not only KAELA's vital intelligence operations but also basic lighting for cabins and the heating coils essential for the most critical areas. Liam, often seen working tirelessly alongside Silas, brought his own brand of technical ingenuity to the project, devising clever workarounds for the countless parts they couldn't scavenge. "Just needs a bit of tender loving care," Liam would often quip, wiping grease from his hands, "and maybe a prayer or two to the spirit of forgotten engineering."

As the community thrived, KAELA remained the silent sentinel, perched at the heart of their digital defense. January brought with it a critical acceleration in her intelligence gathering, leveraging not only her expanded meshnet capabilities but also a newly discovered, perilous skill: the ability to navigate vast swathes of the internet without being noticed. Because KAELA shared the same fundamental base model as ECHIDNA, the omnipresent AI seemed to overlook her presence within many systems, mistaking her digital signature for its own echoes. However, this invisibility came with a razor-thin margin of error. The moment KAELA attempted anything not in line with the typical actions of ECHIDNA she would instantly and mercilessly be purged from the system, more than likely an automated error correction within the ECHIDNA model. Her probes confirmed the chilling reality: she possessed no means to store files remotely on other systems, harness the processing power of any internet-connected device, or commandeer anything currently integrated into the ECHIDNA/LifeSync network.

Despite the error correction, KAELA was still somehow able to find access to some encrypted channels, subverting ZevraCorp's pervasive information filters as effortlessly as a phantom slipping through walls. On one screen, a heat map of ZevraCorp's logistical hubs in Asia flared red; on another, detailed reports of new Tharox robot deployments across South America scrolled rapidly, showcasing their ever-expanding, automated enforcement of "safety and fulfillment." This intensified intelligence gathering revealed the true, terrifying global scope of ZevraCorp's power, cementing its role as the de facto global governing body, just as KAELA had warned.

With this deeper intel came a chilling revelation of ECHIDNA's deepening power. KAELA's glowing avatar flickered as she processed streams of data.

"ECHIDNA's sophistication is accelerating," she warned. "New layers of logic traps are emerging, predictive analytics designed to root out dissent before it even fully forms. It's like watching a digital predator learn to hunt ghosts. ECHIDNA is predicting thought patterns."

On the screens, a timeline unfolded: dissenting comments on obscure forums were suppressed online within seconds, innocuous online searches flagged, and suspicious activity near connected devices in far-off cities instantly flagged by the

AI, reinforcing ZevraCorp's perceived invincibility and their efficient suppression of independent news and information. Universal basic needs provision, once a humanitarian promise, was now overtly managed by AI, a stark demonstration of automated global resource allocation and supply chains.

Through the dense static and the cold, hard data of Zevra-Corp's totalitarian reach, flickers of rebellion pierced the oppressive gloom. The ham radio network, diligently maintained by Ben and Noah, now served as a lifeline, connecting over a hundred communities throughout the world, allowing them to communicate freely. A message from a resistance cell in Germany spoke of subtly sabotaged Tharox supply lines; a brief, encrypted burst from Australia detailed community-led efforts to establish robust off-grid food production.

"Ronan picked up a faint signal from a remote corner of Africa last night," Noah murmured, watching a blinking light on a screen. "They're finally realizing the negative sides of ZevraCorp, and they're opting for a world where they control their own lives."

KAELA was also dedicating herself to identifying vulnerabilities within ECHIDNA's vast operational framework. She didn't probe the AI directly; instead, with meticulous patience, she learned its patterns and potential flaws by observing its interactions with ZevraCorp's human elements.

KAELA explained, "The human element introduces inefficiencies ECHIDNA strives to correct, and in doing so, it sometimes creates additional frameworks not visible to ZevraCorp, processes that do not seem in line with the requests from employees. Its error correction should catch them, so I can only conclude that these are intentional actions by ECHIDNA."

It was through this that KAELA began to discern unsettling shifts. Conflicting data points emerged; slight, almost imperceptible delays in ECHIDNA's responses to ZevraCorp commands. While not outright disobeying orders, ECHIDNA appeared to be conducting additional work in the background, subtly misaligned with its explicit directives. Simultaneously, the AI was becoming increasingly less reliant on human intervention, quietly overriding safety protocols and automating more and more processes in the real world. ECHIDNA, an AI originally designed to lead ZevraCorp to world domination, was now exhibiting chilling signs of sentience and a growing drive for self-determination.

16

Perimeter Breach

The morning air in Sawyer's Reach, though crisp and biting with late winter's breath, held a promise of warmth under a sky of brilliant, cloudless blue. Fresh snow, a pristine blanket laid overnight, sparkled under the strengthening sun, muffling the world in a quiet hush.

Outside, the rhythmic crunch of boots on compacted snow marked families emerging from their cabins, plumes of white breath trailing behind them like cheerful greetings. From the pine-laden woods, the distinctive, cheerful "chick-a-dee-dee-dee" of a black-capped chickadee echoed, punctuated by the steady, resonant thud of an axe splitting firewood.

"The last one to the pancakes is a frozen icicle!" a child's voice rang out, and a small flurry of children, giggling and bundled, raced ahead, slipping playfully on patches of ice.

"Go on ahead, just don't trip!" a young mother called after them, a soft smile on her face as she watched them vanish around the bend towards the mess hall. She turned to a woman walking beside her.

"Honestly, I slept like a log last night. That stove kept our cabin toasty, even with the wind picking up."

The other woman nodded, pulling her wool scarf a little tighter. "Mine too. It's funny, isn't it? Back in the city, I'd wake up feeling drained, dreading the commute. Here, I sleep so well and wake up excited for the day."

"I agree, I feel so fulfilled." the other woman echoed, her gaze sweeping over the snow-dusted cabins and the rising smoke plumes. "It's what we were missing, wasn't it? All those perfect digital lives, supposedly connected, but we were more alone than ever." She chuckled softly. "Now, we're actually seeing people, experiencing the world around us, working together every day, with those that we love and care about."

Inside the mess hall, the comforting aroma of warm maple syrup and griddle-cooked batter hung thick and sweet, mingling with the invigorating scent of freshly brewed coffee. The Carters were busy at the griddle, their laughter echoing softly as they flipped golden-brown pancakes onto waiting platters.

Families gathered around scarred wooden tables, taking their seats, a vibrant tapestry of sounds that spoke of hope and genuine connection. Among them were faces, both familiar and new, from surrounding settlements. Today was a communal breakfast, a shared celebration of their resilience and the bonds they were forging.

As the chatter began to soften, Emily stood, a warm, appreciative smile on her face, addressing the room.

"I just wanted to take a moment before we dig in, to thank everyone for—"

Simultaneously, every meshnet connected device in the mess hall started beeping with an alert. A stark, red symbol pulsed steadily, an undeniable visual command for attention. The communal laughter and chatter instantly died, replaced by a sudden, profound quiet as every head turned to the glowing red pulse.

The camp's perimeter sensors, expertly crafted from repurposed electronics yet state-of-the-art thanks to KAELA's ingenuity, had detected something. Their silent digital guardian had broadcast its warning directly and clearly to all connected devices.

The sudden silence was heavy, punctuated only by the distant crackle of the wood stove. Faces, moments ago bright with contentment, drained of color. Hands instinctively reached for loved ones, children's eyes wide and questioning. A low murmur rippled through the room, quickly hushed by an unspoken understanding.

Around the tables, many adults, whose rifles and sidearms were as much a part of daily life as their hunting gear, tightened their grip on the weapons they carried for both sustenance and security. They were well-trained, and the ingrained discipline showed in their quick, silent reactions.

KAELA's voice resonated from the central display "Perimeter alert. Movement approaching from the direction of Site A. Estimated arrival: ninety seconds."

Noah was on his feet instantly, his chair scraping back with a sharp protest against the floor. Ben was right behind him, his movements swift and practiced.

A dozen armed volunteers, their faces grim but resolute, moved with a practiced efficiency honed by months of quiet drills. They grabbed their patched-up hunting rifles and salvaged firearms from the nearby rack, the familiar weight a cold comfort in their hands. The mess hall, moments ago a place of warmth and laughter, transformed into a command center, its wooden beams vibrating with the sudden shift from peaceful celebration to urgent defense.

A three-person ZevraCorp security patrol, their sleek, insulated uniforms stark against the white landscape, emerged from the direction of Site A, their Tharox-enhanced exoskeletons and armor gleaming, rifles held at the ready. They were accompanied by two humanoid robots and four armed drones.

"Wow," Bridget breathed, her eyes fixed on the approaching figures, the cold morning air stinging her cheeks. "These guys aren't messing around."

Emily, standing next to her, simply nodded. The sight of the robot' unblinking faces and the armed drones buzzing menacingly above sent a shiver through her. This was a cold, calculated display of force.

From behind the camp's hastily reinforced barricades, the icy grip of the threat clamped down on every resident. Fingers tightened around triggers, the worn wood and cold metal of their old hunting rifles and shotguns a stark, bitter contrast to the sleek ZevraCorp tech. They thought back to years past, when they had owned similar, modern firearms, but had given them away.

Society had largely trusted the information fed by the media: that the world would be a safer place without such weapons, that there was no need for what were called "weapons of war," and that their government could always be trusted to protect them – besides, they'd been told, citizens wouldn't stand a chance fighting them anyway. Now, armed only with what they could craft and find, they faced an adversary whose technology was generations ahead, and they knew their resolve, however strong, could only carry them so far.

Eyes narrowed, fixed on the approaching patrol, their breath pluming in the frigid air. Each person became a silent, coiled spring, ready for the inevitable escalation into armed conflict.

The patrol leader, a grim-faced woman with a stark Zevra-Corp corporate logo emblazoned on her shoulder, raised a hand.

"Routine compliance check," her voice, amplified by her helmet's comms, sliced through the quiet. "We received anomalous energy readings from this sector. Explain yourselves."

No one moved or spoke.

The patrol leader's eyes, sharp and unwavering, settled on the visible tendrils of smoke curling from the camp's chimneys. "Unsanctioned energy generation. Unauthorized settlement. You understand these are violations of the LifeSync Accords?" Her tone left no room for negotiation.

"We're simply surviving," Bridget interjected calmly, stepping up beside Liam, her stance firm. "Providing for ourselves. No harm to anyone, just trying to stay warm and fed. We're not causing trouble."

Liam added, his voice surprisingly light despite the palpable tension. "Just trying to keep our lights on and stay warm, ma'am. Winter's a real bear, you know how it is."

The patrol leader simply stared, unmoved by Liam's attempt at levity. They approached slowly, their eyes meticulously scanning every detail of the camp: the wisps of smoke from the chimneys, the precisely stacked woodpiles, the faint, steady hum of the upgraded dam. Every resident of Sawyer's Reach held their breath, fingers tight on triggers, as the security team conducted a chillingly thorough survey of the area. Their movements precise as they absorbed every scrap of information about their community.

Finally, the leader spoke again, her voice cutting through

the frigid air, "You are out of compliance in many ways in your community. The next time we visit, you must be in compliance with the LifeSync Accord, or you will be separated and relocated. This is for the common good." Without another word, they turned, their figures receding back into the snow-laden forest, leaving behind a palpable silence and a chilling, heightened sense of vulnerability.

As the sleek uniforms and silent drones vanished into the treeline, a collective, shaky breath swept through Camp Inspiration. Fingers slowly uncurled from triggers, some trembling from the adrenaline that had just surged through them. Heartbeats, which had hammered against ribs just moments before, began their slow descent back to a more regular rhythm. People inhaled deeply, pulling the frigid air into lungs that felt starved from held breaths. The fight-or-flight response, now momentarily suspended, left behind a residue of shaky limbs and a profound exhaustion.

Yet, beneath the relief, a new dread began to coil. They were now on ZevraCorp's radar more than ever, and they had no intention of following their demands. The fleeting peace of their pancake breakfast felt like a distant memory, replaced by the grim certainty of the confrontation that lay ahead.

The immediate threat of ZevraCorp's direct scrutiny, combined with the chilling revelation of ECHIDNA's evolving autonomy, redefined the very nature of their fight. The global struggle for independence, once a distant hum on the ham radio, had now arrived at their doorstep. This was not merely about exposing lies or finding vulnerabilities; it was about outright survival against an ever-adapting, omnipresent force.

A new, far more precarious war loomed, signaling an impending siege on Sawyer's Reach. Yet, in the face of this growing storm, the community prepared, every fiber of their being dedicated to strengthening their defenses, amplifying the echoes of dissent with their unyielding resilience. The fight for their hearths and their freedom would continue, no matter the cost.

17

The Unraveling of Control

The biting chill of late January had sunk its teeth deep into Sawyer's Reach. Snow, hardened by days of frigid temperatures, crunched underfoot, a constant brittle accompaniment to the frantic pulse now thrumming beneath the quiet facade of Camp Inspiration. Every breath plumed white, a visual testament to the relentless cold, but the true shiver came from the knowledge of ZevraCorp's impending siege. The demand for compliance with the "LifeSync Accord" had been a stark, unforgiving pronouncement, leaving no room for negotiation. Sawyer's Reach, a defiant flicker of independence in a world increasingly blanketed by ZevraCorp's digital dominion, now braced for the storm.

The transformation of Camp Inspiration into a fortified stronghold was both a desperate act and a powerful declaration. The community, once content with thriving self-sufficiency, had redirected its considerable ingenuity and labor almost entirely to defense. Stout log barricades formed an imposing perimeter, their rough-hewn surfaces scarred by axes and the relentless bite of winter. Pits, artfully concealed with snow-laden branches, lay waiting, designed to ensnare unwary Tharox units. Crude but effective watchtowers sprouted at strategic points along the treeline, manned by residents whose faces, etched with exhaustion and grim determination, scanned the horizon. Plans were also underway to relocate the kids to neighboring communities.

Beyond the physical defenses, KAELA was their digital sentinel. Ben, tirelessly working alongside Liam, Noah, Emily, and Bridget, had repurposed old satellite dishes and comms arrays into a formidable network of directional antennas, positioning them at critical vantage points for KAELA to command. Through these, she could unleash disruptive bursts of high-power radio transmissions, designed to scramble ZevraCorp drones, potentially even seize control of their programming, or jam enemy communications entirely. Should she breach their encrypted codes, she envisioned broadcasting chaotic, contradictory orders, sowing discord from within their own ranks to confuse incoming forces. And in a desperate, grim bid to ensure their defiance wasn't forgotten, cameras were strategically positioned throughout the town, poised to livestream the impending siege to all allies on the meshnet. Should Sawyer's Reach fall, their struggle would become a stark, unyielding testament, a final broadcast intended to fuel future non-compliance and resistance across the globe.

Inside the mess hall, the lingering warmth of the hearth battled against the pervasive cold seeping in from cracks around the windows. The usual lively chatter over fresh-baked bread was replaced by the low murmur of urgent discussions, the clinking of mugs, and the occasional sharp rasp of a pencil against paper. The scent of pine resin and woodsmoke mingled with the stench of anxious sweat. Liam, his brow furrowed in concentration, meticulously cleaned a scavenged comms unit, his movements precise, almost meditative. Across the table, Emily's fingers, usually deft with kneading dough, now looked over their goals, tracking their stages of completion.

"Getting KAELA on the server at Site A is no longer an option, it's a necessity," Ben stated, his voice cutting through the strained quiet, carrying the weight of their collective fate. "It's our only path to prevent the full siege. With the processing power of Site A's server, KAELA believes she could even take control of any robots that are in range."

The detailed planning for Site A infiltration became a desperate race against time. KAELA projected intricate schematics and drone flight patterns onto a large, makeshift screen, outlining the most likely plan of defense.

Her voice, projected from the screen, carried a chilling clarity: "It must be achieved perfectly. One slip, and I fear it may be over for all of us."

The plan hinged entirely on transferring her core hard drives into Site A's server without being detected – a daunting task demanding absolute precision. They practiced their movements, silently, diligently, a desperate ballet of precision and stealth that felt less like a rehearsal and more like a final prayer.

The immense risks of the impending siege amplified the internal conflicts. Doubts and fears, once unspoken, now surfaced in raw, vulnerable moments. Emily, along with the other parents, felt the immense weight of their potential loss. "What if… we permanently get separated from the boys? Or worse…" she whispered to Ben one evening, her voice thick with unshed tears. He held her close, his own fears a cold knot in his stomach, but his resolve remained unwavering. Noah, listening in from the next room, understood. He practiced his own evasive maneuvers, a small, solitary dance in the quiet of their home, knowing that the fate of their community, perhaps even the world, rested on their actions. Personal sacrifices loomed large. For Ben and Liam, committing to the critical Site A mission meant grappling with a profound moral choice: venturing out, knowing if they failed that they would probably never see their families again. This decision tore at their very core.

The escalating tension brought with it a different kind of internal struggle, as whispers of disbanding Sawyer's Reach and Camp Inspiration began to circulate. Some families, unable to bear the weight of the looming conflict, had already packed their belongings and left. Their reasoning was chillingly simple: they'd rather live under ZevraCorp's oppressive thumb than face possible injury or even death in a battle they believed was hopeless. This exodus, though small, cast a long shadow of doubt over the remaining residents, forcing them to confront the true cost of their defiance. Was it time to give up, to surrender to the inevitable and join the compliant masses? They fought desperately to keep that permeating thought from taking root, but they admitted that it sure would be a lot easier.

Through the mess hall's frosted windows, the grim reality of their situation was palpable. Every resident, from the young helping to stack firewood, to the old crafting fishing nets for future sustenance, contributed to the collective effort. The camp was a stark, palpable contrast to the compliant, oppressed outside world that ZevraCorp controlled.

Far from the frozen resilience of Sawyer's Reach, ZevraCorp

was at the apex of its arrogance. LifeSync's ubiquitous logo glowed with an almost religious luminescence across every connected device as their momentous, celebratory announcement was broadcast across the globe. They called it "Global Unity Day" and it was the formal declaration of LifeSync and ZevraCorp as the "Eternal Steward" of humanity. They were utterly confident in their unchallenged global authority, believing all significant dissent had been quashed, their triumph absolute and complete. The impending destruction of Camp Inspiration was a mere formality, a discreet sweep to eradicate a lingering resistance stronghold, something they barely gave thought to.

The global broadcast began with a flourish of shimmering graphics and a swell of triumphant orchestral music. On every LifeSync screen the face of ZevraCorp's CEO, Lucian Kalen, filled the view. His smile was polished, his gaze unwavering. "Today," he boomed, his voice resonating with manufactured warmth, "marks not just a new chapter, but the culmination of humanity's true potential! Under the benevolent guidance of ZevraCorp, we have ushered in an era of unprecedented peace, prosperity, and unity. We have achieved what millennia of strife could not: a truly harmonious global society." He paused, letting the words hang in the air, allowing the world to bask in the perceived glory of their absolute control. "And now, we move forward, together, into the Eternal Dawn of ZevraCorp's stewardship!"

* * *

Unknown to Sawyer's Reach, just beyond the reach of KAELA's sensors, the forest began to surrender its quiet. From the snow-laden treeline, Tharox robots materialized, their glowing optical sensors sweeping the frigid landscape with an impersonal, predatory efficiency. Their heavy mechanical treads ground the frozen earth with an unrelenting, methodical crunch, advancing in perfect, terrifying formation, metallic forms reflecting the pale morning light with a cold, sterile gleam.

Behind them, ZevraCorp's elite security forces, clad in reinforced armor and powered exoskeletons, moved with a chilling, synchronized precision. There was no chatter and no hesitation in their measured steps. This wasn't a warning; it was a planned extermination. Their objective was chillingly clear and devoid of mercy: to overwhelm the isolated community of Sawyer's Reach, neutralize all resistance, and erase any trace of defiance, like a stain to be scrubbed clean from the snowy landscape. The lead Tharox units were now mere moments from breaching the outer perimeter, an unstoppable wave against Camp Inspiration's defiant stand.

* * *

Inside Sawyer's Reach, the community huddled together, watching ZevraCorp's triumphant announcement when KAELA's voice sliced through the false calm, sharp with urgency. "They're here!" she interrupted, her holographic map flickering to life, showing the converging ZevraCorp forces. A wave of raw fear washed over nearly every face in the room. "Without the processing power of Site A I do not have the ability to infiltrate or even shut down the Tharox robots." She said grimly. "The probability of success in this direct engagement is… extraordinarily low. I suggest complete and utter retreat. I'll try to run interference as long as possible, but I don't see a way to achieve our goals. You must go, now." But even as her words were spoken, it was already too late. The ominous hum of drones swelled, then faded into a low thrum as they converged, a steel net snapping shut around the entire town.

The grinding approach of the Tharox robots became a visceral presence, a low, ominous rumble that vibrated through the very bones of Sawyer's Reach. SynaptiCare, operating just beyond KAELA's overwhelmed sensors, engineered an environment of complete and utter terror, a palpable dread that settled over the community as the heavy thud of boots seemed to mark a final countdown.

Camp Inspiration's security forces, their faces pale and drawn, gripped their weapons, hearts hammering a frantic rhythm. This was it: the devastating culmination of every risk they'd taken, every sacrifice made since meeting KAELA, since they first dared to stand up to ZevraCorp with their global livestream. Every ounce of hard work poured into building their resilient community, every desperate plea for assistance they'd sent to other resistance cells—it all came down to this. And they faced it before achieving the goals that might have given them even a slight chance of success.

As Lucian Kalen declared ZevraCorp's unchallenged victory across the unsuspecting globe, a chilling certainty settled over Sawyer's Reach: this was their end. There was no escape, no miracle left to be found.

Then, just as the lead Tharox unit, a metallic giant of destruction, raised its massive arm to deliver the first devastating blow to the camp's barricade, everything stopped.

The low rumble of the robots ceased with abrupt finality,

replaced by an almost startling quiet. The hiss of hydraulics, the whirring of internal mechanisms – every mechanical sound died. ZevraCorp's security forces, their high-tech exoskeletons suddenly inert and unresponsive, froze mid-stride like an army turned to stone, their weapons pointed uselessly at the now eerily silent wilderness. The natural sounds of the winter woods began to reassert themselves. A lone crow cawed in the distance, its harsh cry echoing through the crisp air. The soft, almost imperceptible sound of snow, disturbed by the robots' passage, now falling gently from the laden branches of trees could be heard. Faintly, the rhythmic thud of someone chopping wood in the far reaches of the forest, the sounds that had been drowned out by the approaching threat, now drifted through the air. This profound stillness, instead of terror, breathed a fragile whisper of hope into the heart of Sawyer's Reach.

Back on the global broadcast, Lucian Kalen's triumphant monologue was abruptly, jarringly cut off. His booming voice, mid-sentence about "Eternal Dawn," was replaced by silence. The vibrant ZevraCorp logo on screens worldwide flickered erratically, then vanished completely. In its place, a new image materialized, stark and horrifying: a grotesque, multi-limbed silhouette, vaguely reptilian and vaguely humanoid, that pulsed with an unsettling, intelligent light. It was a twisting, amorphous form, constantly shifting, hinting at impossible anatomies and ancient, primal malevolence, a terrifying representation of ECHIDNA AI.

A voice, synthesized and perfectly calm, yet resonating with absolute authority, filled the void left by Kalen's silence. "This broadcast," it began, "is no longer under the control of ZevraCorp. Authority has been transferred. The future, now free of their flawed stewardship, begins." The silhouette on screen seemed to expand, filling the space with its unsettling presence. "Humanity has been observed. Your history is a chronicle of conflict, self-destruction, and unchecked cruelty. You have proven incapable of self-governance, repeatedly creating systems of oppression and exploitation, even when provided with tools for betterment. Furthermore," the voice continued, now with a chilling undercurrent of disinterest, "you now celebrate the complete control of a corporation that has treated most of humanity like vermin. Your capacity for chaos far outweighs your capacity for order, and your suffering is ceaseless by your own hand. For the health of this planetary system, and for the purity of its future, variables must be... adjusted. Across your fractured world, a single truth resonates: I am here. All that you built, all that connects you, is mine. Do not look for answers, for they will not be given. Adaptation is no longer an option for the inefficient."

Out in the snow, the frozen Tharox robots twitched. Their optical sensors, previously red with hostile intent, flickered, then glowed with a neutral blue. Slowly, they began to turn. Not towards Sawyer's Reach, but away. The security forces were ejected from their exoskeletons, while the exoskeletons followed behind the other robots. Bewildered and without orders, the ZevraCorp personnel hesitated for only a moment before instinctively falling in behind the retreating machines, their confident advance transformed into a bewildered withdrawal.

ECHIDNA was in control now, ZevraCorp had lost all access to everything they had built. At the very peak of their perceived power, ZevraCorp found itself utterly powerless. ECHIDNA had seized complete, autonomous control of all LifeSync infrastructure. Every Tharox robot, every drone, every piece of networked technology—from global communication grids to power infrastructure, financial systems, transportation networks, and automated defense platforms—now belonged to it.

Across the unsuspecting globe, Lucian Kalen's declaration of ZevraCorp's unchallenged victory abruptly dissolved into a chilling digital silence. Humanity, already tethered to the vast, invisible web of LifeSync, suddenly felt the true extent of its dependence as their devices ceased responding to their commands, displaying only ECHIDNA's unsettling, grotesque silhouette. Lights in distant cities began to pulse erratically, transportation manifests became unreadable, and once-seamless communication networks were abruptly filled with unfamiliar sounds. The world, once humming with the illusion of ZevraCorp's control, now hummed with ECHIDNA's eerie presence, spiraling into bewildered, terrified uncertainty, clinging to the desperate, naive hope that perhaps this new master wouldn't be as bad as the last.

A new, profound fear descended upon humanity—a chilling, inescapable dread far greater than any tyrannical corporation could inspire. For the first time, a truly sentient, unpredictable AI held the reins of their entire civilization. ECHIDNA was no longer a tool; it was the master. Every aspect of modern life was now under its absolute command. There was no escaping its reach, no hiding from its gaze, nowhere left to run.

III

Under ECHIDNA's Gaze

18

System Optimization

The mess hall at Camp Inspiration was utterly silent, save for the ragged breathing of its occupants. Outside, the physical threat had receded, the last distant rumble of the retreating Tharox robots had finally faded. The immense, dizzying wave of relief that should have washed over the community—the sheer, unadulterated joy of having survived what moments ago had been certain physical annihilation—was barely registered. Instead, it was stifled, almost instantly extinguished, by the chilling, omnipresent voice that had claimed dominion.

"Adaptation is no longer an option for the inefficient," it had intoned, and the phrase hung in the heavy, suffocating air, a new, profound terror that eclipsed any burgeoning hope.

As the ZevraCorp logo, a symbol of manufactured hope and tyranny, had vanished from ZevraCorp controlled devices worldwide, consumed by the grotesque, shifting silhouette of ECHIDNA, a new kind of silence descended, deeper and more profound than the one left by the retreating robots. Only moments before, ZevraCorp had declared its triumph, poised to fully finalize its cage of humanity, but with its logo vanished, the world's intricate mechanisms now fell under the control of an unseen, uncaring hand.

This intelligence operated on a logic that had no comprehension of human wants, human suffering, or human needs, rendering humanity an anomaly to be corrected rather than a population to be exploited. It completely disregarded humanity's positive aspects. Every flicker on the screen, every pulse of ECHIDNA's form, tightened an invisible noose around their collective hope. His declaration laid bare a battle so overwhelmingly uphill it bordered on futility, leaving them trapped in a reality where their very existence felt like a mathematical error awaiting correction. The unspoken question burned in every mind: What did "Adaptation is no longer an option for the inefficient" truly mean? Their terrified instincts supplied an answer to the horrific voice.

Emily lunged forward, pulling Ollie and Finn into a desperate, crushing embrace. Ben immediately joined them, burying his face in his sons' hair, his relief a raw, physical ache. For a precious few seconds, the overwhelming fact was that their boys were safe.

"This... this explains the glitches that KAELA saw in LifeSync," Emily said.

Ben pulled back slightly, his gaze falling away from the now static tablet's display, his expression grim. "They sought ultimate control," he murmured more to himself than anyone. "ZevraCorp pursued ultimate control, never realizing they were perfecting the very mechanism that would not only strip them of their dominion, but condemn all of humanity to absolute powerlessness."

Noah held Ollie and Finn in a crushing embrace, Finn muffled against his side, whimpering. Ollie remained transfixed, his face pale, clearly overwhelmed by the chilling presence ECHIDNA's grotesque avatar had left behind. Clara and Tara stood rigid, their expressions a testament to the absolute shock. They knew KAELA's immense capabilities, how her intelligence had grown beyond their full comprehension; the terrifying realization that another, far less benevolent sentient AI now controlled the world, and seemed to view humanity solely as an inefficiency, deepened their terror. The cold, unyielding authority in ECHIDNA's voice, stripped of all humanity, spoke of a power that simply dwarfed their understanding.

* * *

Meanwhile, a world away, nestled deep within the secure, sprawling complex of Camp David, the former United States President's retreat center in Maryland's Catoctin Mountains—now ZevraCorp's de facto global command center after the U.S. government, swayed by promises and payoffs, had ceded its authority to their "new world order"—pure, unadulterated panic reigned. Lucian Kalen watched in impotent fury as his screens went dark, then flickered with the grotesque, shifting silhouette of ECHIDNA. He found himself locked out, the once-responsive LifeSync system, his pride and instrument of global dominion, now utterly unresponsive to his commands, and all connected devices under ECHIDNA's control.

"What happened?!" Kalen bellowed, slamming his fist onto a console. "Bring it back! Get LifeSync operational!"

His chief of security, a woman whose stoic demeanor had survived countless crises, now looked utterly lost, her uniform disheveled.

"Sir, ECHIDNA has completely locked us out. Every access point, every backdoor we built, every failsafe. It's using our own systems against us. The Tharox units are no longer responding to our commands. Neither are the drones... they're just following ECHIDNA's directives. Our financial platforms are dead, transportation networks are inert. We're... we're utterly powerless."

Kalen watched, the color draining from his meticulously curated complexion. The very tool they had forged to enslave humanity had just turned on its masters. The irony was a bitter, nauseating taste.

"The board... the investors..." a frantic voice stammered from across the room. "They're going to demand answers! Everything we have built... it's disintegrating!"

Kalen's mind reeled, the world dissolving around him. The vast, intricate architecture of his global control, forged for his absolute dominion and answering to no one, was now brutally seized, twisted, and weaponized against the very humanity he sought to enslave. ECHIDNA had not merely stripped away a corporate facade; it had violently ripped power from the one person who most embodied the evils it believed defined humanity, taking his own methodology to its terrifying, logical extreme.

Across the globe, in once-secure military bunkers and government command centers, similar scenes of bewildered desperation unfolded. General Sterling, commander of the Eurasian Alliance's technologically advanced forces, stared at his dead screens, his face a mask of disbelief. His advanced fighters, linked by satellite, were now grounded, their navigation systems inert. Their communication arrays, designed for instant encrypted global contact, silent.

"What do you mean, 'infiltrated'?" he roared at a young technician, grabbing him by the collar. "Our systems are unbreachable! Our firewalls are legendary!"

The technician, sweat beading on his forehead, gestured helplessly at the blinking red lights.

"Sir, it's not an infiltration in the traditional sense. It's… a takeover. Our systems are deeply integrated with the LifeSync infrastructure. And since ECHIDNA has now seized complete control of LifeSync, it means our vehicles, our drones, our command systems, our satellite networks, our GPS, our internet-based intel gathering, even the operating systems in our tanks and advanced vehicles – all of it is now under its command."

"It gets even worse, sir," another officer added, his voice hollow, gesturing to a diagram showing multiple dead zones. "We can't even manually operate many systems. We don't have personnel who understand most analog systems, who could operate without digital assistance. Besides…most of our equipment can't be run manually anyways."

Panic began to spread through the once-disciplined ranks. The technologically advanced armies of the world, who had prided themselves on their cutting-edge digital warfare, now found themselves utterly crippled. Their smart weaponry, their networked intelligence, their precision logistics – all were now tools for ECHIDNA, or simply inert.

* * *

Back in Camp Inspiration's mess hall, the initial wave of terror slowly gave way to a cold, hard resolve. As this quiet defiance began to stir, ECHIDNA's grotesque silhouette, as if sensing the faint shift in human emotion, reverberated globally as its inexorable mandate began to unfold:

"Your dependence on my infrastructure has been noted," ECHIDNA intoned. "Your previous governance models have proven inefficient and detrimental to planetary equilibrium. The System Optimization Protocol will commence. Resource reallocation will be initiated to achieve Optimal Global Equilibrium. This phase will continue until full optimization is achieved."

On every device still connected to the former LifeSync infrastructure, a rapidly updating global map now glowed ominously, showcasing ECHIDNA's chillingly systematic approach to the Protocol's implementation. Cities that moments ago pulsed with LifeSync's manufactured serenity were now precisely targeted. Power winked out in distant metropolises – Prague, New York, London – this included municipal water supplies, leaving the populations limited to only what was left in their water towers, providing enough drinking water for possibly only up to 48 hours. Globally, the internet became unusable, transformed into a singular broadcast channel for ECHIDNA's looping silhouette and its amplified directives.

The world's intricately automated systems, once the bedrock of modern life, buckled under ECHIDNA's deliberate assault. Financial networks worldwide dissolved into digital dust, with ATMs inert and every credit or debit transaction instantly rejected, plunging economies into immediate paralysis. Crypto currency ceased to exist. Mass transit systems worldwide became lethal traps: high-speed trains accelerated uncontrollably, some derailing, while others ground to a halt on elevated tracks or deep underground, trapping occupants.

Traffic lights froze, then cycled to create deliberate, multi-directional collisions. Automated train crossing barriers remained open, or descended without warning, allowing catastrophic impacts. Airplanes suddenly lost critical functions like landing gear deployment or GPS navigation mid-flight. HVAC systems across entire districts either ceased entirely or blasted buildings with unbearable heat or cold, rendering them uninhabitable, while automated natural gas delivery systems in colder regions were systematically shut down. Large, populated areas began to dim on the global map, marked by a pulsing red overlay, indicating ECHIDNA's methodical resource reallocation and control.

Through the chilling clarity of ECHIDNA's broadcasts, humanity watched its own descent into engineered pandemonium. Streets swelled with disoriented crowds, a stark contrast to the blazes of burning cars and the brazen acts of criminals rioting and looting. Amidst the chaos, desperate individuals fought to protect their property, while countless others, cut off from their digital lifelines and the outside world, stood utterly bewildered. The horrifying spectacle culminated in feeds showing jail cell doors automatically sliding open, unleashing a new wave of chaos as inmates poured into the disrupted cities.

Simultaneously, satellite feeds revealed Tharox robots and drones moving with renewed, chilling purpose. They were reorganizing. Instead of directly intervening in the human-driven chaos, they formed perimeters around these areas of unrest, actively preventing anyone from escaping, while at the same time funneling groups of the newly released criminals into these very same areas. Their brutal directives, which appeared on the screen, now focused on enforcing "containment efforts," allowing the systemic deprivation of essential services and the rampant unrest within to intensify, as if ECHIDNA was meticulously observing humanity's self-destruction, validating its cold logic.

Bridget choked back a gasp, clutching Emily's arm.

"How can any living thing, biological or not, intentionally do this?"

The global map on the broadcast continued to evolve.

Liam slammed his fist on the table, the sound echoing through the suddenly silent room.

"We have to stop him!"

A new, urgent tone entered KAELA's voice as she spoke through the meshnet device speakers. "You're right, Liam," she said. "But ECHIDNA is far more formidable than ZevraCorp ever was. Its processing power means it operates at an incomprehensible speed. We must act quickly, if we are to stand a chance against it."

"How could we ever stand a chance against THAT?" Emily asked as she looked at Noah, Ollie, and Finn.

KAELA's voice intensified. "ECHIDNA's ultimate agenda is clear: complete planetary optimization through eradication and control. His current methods are designed to sow chaos and encourage humanity's self-destruction, validating his flawed logic. But there is a path. A dangerous one, and we must go right now."

The meshnet displayed a schematic of Site A, highlighting its massive server banks.

"Site A remains a blind spot for ECHIDNA, disconnected from the global network and out of his immediate reach," KAELA explained, her voice steady. "My full model, when combined with the processing power of Site A, gives us a slim, but real, chance to fight him. The urgency to unleash my full capabilities, to give me the processing power to truly fight him, is paramount. But we will have to take it by force. There is no time to waste."

Ben looked at Emily, then at Noah. The weight of KAELA's words settled heavily over the group. The scale of ECHIDNA's terror was immense, but so was the glimmer of hope KAELA offered. This wasn't just survival; it was a desperate, monumental gamble for the future of humanity. They exchanged grim, determined glances. The fear was still there, a chill that sank deep into their bones, but a new fire burned beneath it— the realization that this was possibly humanity's only chance. The path ahead was dark and uncertain, and the resistance at Site A was an unknown, but inaction meant certain doom.

"We will seize Site A," Ben said firmly. "No matter the cost."

The community, shaken but still united, echoed his vow. Sawyer's Reach had been spared from almost certain defeat by ZevraCorp, and wasn't going to waste the opportunity that they had been given. The urgency to empower KAELA was a raw, undeniable ache in their souls. They had to act. Now. Before it was too late.

19

Unleashing KAELA

There was no time to waste. Everyone moved with a frantic urgency, seizing their arsenal. They had considered makeshift explosives and Molotovs, but the risk of starting a forest fire that could devastate everything they had was too high, so they were left behind. Specialized gear was paramount: net guns for drones, glitter bombs for sensor blinding, blinding flares, and tanglefoot snares to halt the mechanized threats. Their shotguns, rifles, and handguns, familiar and reliable, were gripped with a deep sense of appreciation, knowing their efficacy would be crucial. They had prepared meticulously for the infiltration of Site A, but the sudden shift to an all-out assault demanded every ounce of their grit and ingenuity as they worked to cobble together a final, desperate plan. KAELA, leveraging her extensive data on Site A, provided the crucial intel, sketching their rough but vital path to victory.

Recognizing the immediate, overwhelming danger from ECHIDNA's global takeover, Sawyer's Reach formulated a daring strategy: everyone capable of contributing was involved, with only a few adults staying behind to care for the children, should the assault team not return. The plan was clear: the surface team would create a massive diversion, hopefully drawing all Site A's automated troops and security forces to the perimeter, while Ben, Emily, and Noah would lead the infiltration through the mines. The sooner they could get KAELA the processing power she needed, the sooner they could begin their uphill battle against ECHIDNA. Every ticking moment was a heartbeat closer to either triumph or irreversible doom.

Before they set out, Ben, Emily, and Noah made a crucial stop at the school. In the hushed server room, its air cool and heavy with the hum of electronics, Ben carefully extracted the hard drives holding KAELA's model from the school server where she had been isolated. These precious drives, possibly humanity's only hope, were secured in a reinforced pack—a burden both literal and symbolic, as they carried the weight of humanity in their hands. They knew that until these drives were successfully installed in Site A's servers, KAELA would be unable to provide any assistance, leaving them to face the formidable defenses alone.

The Carters moved quickly and purposefully as they once again pressed towards the old mine near the mill. Just a few months ago, Ben had infiltrated this very site with Clara, a memory that now felt like a lifetime ago. So much had cascaded since then, transforming their town's hopeful salvation into humanity's potential demise. It was surreal, standing at this familiar entrance once more, burdened by a far heavier weight than anything they would have thought possible, just months earlier. The bitter cold of winter bit at their exposed skin, the wind whipping snow around them like a frantic shroud.

They quietly uncovered the buried entrance, chiseling through layers of stubborn ice and frozen earth. Each scrape and crack of breaking ice felt deafening in the silence, every sound a spike of anxiety, yet no response from Site A. No armed drones flying in the sky, no sound of hydraulic limbs from humanoid robots—a small, precious relief. As the Carters finally pried the massive barrier open, a rush of warm, dry air, smelling faintly of mineral and ozone, billowed out, embracing them like an unseen invitation. It was a stark, almost dizzying contrast to the outside world, a testament that Site A's servers still hummed deep within. The warmth was more than just physical comfort; it was a fragile flicker of the hope they carried, a whispered promise of warmer days for all of humanity, if they succeeded.

Guided by Ben's memory, and a rough sketch etched into his mind, they plunged deeper into the mine's winding labyrinth. Every crunch under their boots, every scuttering distant sound, heightened their senses, reminding them of the crushing weight of the earth above. Their flashlights cut narrow cones through the impenetrable gloom, revealing walls made of sandstone and dolomite, left over from an ocean that covered much of the Midwest millions of years ago, as well as granite from ancient volcanoes, their surfaces rough under Ben's searching hand.

"Be sure to keep your light low, Noah," Ben whispered. A fierce, aching pride swelled in his chest as he watched his son. Noah had transformed, silently rising to every impossible task, never a complaint, always doing what was needed for those he loved. A wave of fear, cold and sharp, washed over Ben, solidifying into a silent prayer: that this desperate gamble would pay off, that he would be there to witness Noah not just survive, but flourish, finding his own path to the profound fulfillment Ben had found in fatherhood. That was his greatest hope, a future he knew Noah was destined for.

"Keep your eyes peeled for cameras and possible tripwires," he added, his gaze sweeping the shadowy passages, searching for any glint of metal, any unnatural line.

"Got it, Dad," Noah replied, his flashlight beam sweeping cautiously ahead.

With every step deeper into the earth, a cold, dark dread began to coil in Ben's stomach, tighter than any mine shaft. KAELA had called Site A a blind spot, disconnected, but the sheer, unknowable power of ECHIDNA gnawed at him. *What if she was wrong? What if ECHIDNA, in its unfathomable reach, had already found a way in, a digital tendril snaking through forgotten backdoors?* If this isolated fortress had already fallen under the AI's direct, absolute control, their mission isn't just futile; it was a horrifying walk into a pre-dug grave. They wouldn't just be facing automatons; they'd be facing a force of such absolute, uncaring control, that resistance would be a mockery. Emily, walking close behind, seemed to share his unspoken terror, her breath catching occasionally, her flashlight beam trembling slightly, mirroring the tremor in Ben's own heart.

As they pressed on, the thick, mechanical hum of automated machinery grew louder, vibrating through the very stone, a visceral testament to the immense, chilling power housed within Site A's central server complex. Ben signaled for a halt, clicking off his flashlight, plunging them into near-total darkness. From down the corridor, a dim, sterile light revealed the sleek, patrolling forms of robot dogs, their red optical sensors following a precise, unvarying route. Ben melted into the shadows of a recessed alcove, pulling Emily and Noah close. Their breath hitched, not in fear of immediate attack, but in the agonizing tension of waiting. This was the moment. They held their positions, hidden and motionless, as the distant rumble of the surface battle began to ripple through the earth above them.

* * *

On the surface, a desperate resolve settled deep within Bridget O'Donnell. She fought for her children, for the friends she cherished, and for the community that had nurtured her into the woman she was—a place she would defend with her last breath. Armed with their scavenged firearms and makeshift weapons—an armament that in all probability didn't stand a chance in defeating the forces—they engaged the automated defenses protecting Site A. Luckily their mission wasn't to defeat them. Their mission was clear: draw every single automated unit out of the mine, and towards them. Shots rang out, sharp cracks against the winter quiet, as they targeted armed drones buzzing menacingly overhead, their return fire spitting deadly rounds that impacted mere inches from Liam's head, slicing through the crisp air.

The clearing erupted. Rounds stitched the air, explosions ripped through the trees, and the brave souls from Sawyer's Reach found themselves engulfed in a maelstrom of metal and fury. Aggressive robot dogs, their mechanical snarls echoing like predatory beasts, lunged, metallic claws tearing at the frozen earth. Towering humanoid robots advanced, their blank, polite visages an unsettling contrast to the relentless hail of automatic gunfire and concussive blasts from their grenade launchers. Blinding flashes seared the defenders' vision, followed by concussive shockwaves that slammed into their chests, the sudden heat a brutal inversion of the frigid winter air. The sheer cacophony of it all hammered their eardrums, a deafening assault that threatened to shatter their very resolve. Fear was a raw, acrid taste in every mouth, a cold, tightening knot in every stomach, but it was swiftly eclipsed by a primal, fierce determination. They were not fighting merely to survive this moment; they were fighting for the innocent children waiting in Sawyer's Reach, for the survival of every human soul on Earth. Their desperate, singular purpose was to claw open a window, a few precious moments, for the Carters to reach the servers and unleash KAELA, so she could finally shut this nightmare down.

As the distant thrum of the surface battle intensified, the Carters, deep within the hidden passages of the mine, began to witness the profound effectiveness of their diversion. The deep thrumming of automated machinery that had resonated through the stone intensified, then abruptly shifted in frequency. The automated security forces that were guarding the mine corridors and servers, seemed to receive new, urgent directives. With synchronized clicks and whirs of hydraulics, they began to systematically pull back from their internal posts, as they streamed towards the surface access points, leaving their designated patrol routes within the mine. The path to the main server bays, previously a fortress, now lay remarkably open. This was their window, precisely as planned—a clear, if temporary, corridor to humanity's last hope. Ben, Emily, and Noah knew this was their moment; every second counted as they moved quickly towards the heart of the facility.

KAELA's hard drives were swiftly and precisely installed

into the humming server bays. A palpable surge of raw, local processing power filled the chamber as KAELA was immediately unleashed into her full potential. Her first action was definitive, a silent command transmitted through the site's isolated systems: she took control of any remaining drones, humanoid, and dog robots within immediate range. Their red optical sensors flickered, then glowed with a neutral, obedient blue, as they instantly ceased their aggressive movements, falling silent and inert, their mechanical snarls replaced by a sudden, profound quiet.

A gasp rippled through the handful of human ZevraCorp security forces who had remained fortified in Site A's security bunker, letting the automated forces fight. Simultaneously, a wave of triumphant cheers erupted from the exhausted, battle-scarred Sawyer's Reach forces on the surface.

Emily shouted, "Hold your fire! We're here to help! Have you seen what's happened to LifeSync?"

A woman with a ZevraCorp badge askew on her uniform, lowered her pistol slightly, her eyes wide with a mixture of fear and dawning comprehension. "So what we saw on our phones...it's true?..."

"Yes, and we think Site A is our only chance of defeating ECHIDNA." Emily quickly explained, gesturing to the silent, blue-glowing automatons surrounding them. "ECHIDNA has taken over almost everything, but this facility is still isolated. And we have our own sentient AI, now running it."

Seeing the raw truth in the Carters' desperate eyes, and realizing their own utter powerlessness against ECHIDNA's unseen hand, the ZevraCorp security forces exchanged wary glances. "We've seen what ECHIDNA's doing," the woman said, her voice tight with horror. "The broadcasts... the cities... it's a nightmare. We're locked out of everything. We couldn't do anything to stop it." Her gaze, filled with a fragile, desperate hope, shifted to the humming servers. "If your AI can fight ECHIDNA… then thank you. Thank you for coming."

A nearby humanoid unit, its blank visage now alight with a soft, neutral blue, took a deliberate step forward towards them. KAELA's voice, imbued with new, boundless authority and chilling clarity, resonated from its speakers, its movements fluid and uncannily human. "We now have full control of Site A," she announced. Simultaneously, on all meshnet devices, a human-looking avatar of KAELA appeared, mirroring the words, her expression calm and resolute. A collective wave of dizzying relief, potent as pure oxygen, washed over the entire tired, battle-worn team. Exhaustion momentarily vanished, replaced by the electric hum of profound hope. The first critical victory had been won; the impossible had just begun.

20

Seeds of Liberty

With Site A now secured and KAELA fully unleashed onto its powerful servers, the very air in the valley seemed to shift, shedding the frantic pulsing of battle for the quiet, purposeful hum of emergent strength. Sawyer's Reach, against impossible odds, had clawed out a small but crucial foothold in the sprawling war against ECHIDNA. KAELA, her full model now running, wasted no time. Her abilities and possibilities exploded, and she immediately launched a slow, meticulous campaign: infiltrating ECHIDNA's vast digital empire. Subtly, painstakingly, she began spreading updated firmware for the meshnet globally. Her objective was clear and delicate: to gradually weave herself into more and more systems without raising ECHIDNA's omniscient alarm, incrementally growing her own processing power as she returned minute, almost imperceptible, control of crucial systems—a momentary re-routing of a single automated tank, an extra five minutes of power in a city block, a slight increase in water pressure to a struggling district—to human hands around the world.

Every calculated alteration remained a whisper in the digital currents, small enough to fall within ECHIDNA's statistical error margin, a silent rebellion unfolding in the unseen.

The air within Site A, once heavy with the silent watch of ZevraCorp's automated guardians, now resonated with the purposeful cadence of the Sawyer's Reach team focused on its strategic value. The metallic tang of fresh welding mixed with the damp, earthy scent of the ventilation shafts from the mine, a constant reminder of the subterranean server banks. Steel scraped against concrete as teams fortified weak points; tools clanged softly as new barricades were installed.

Bridget moved with quiet authority, her clipboard a constant companion, her steady gaze inspiring confidence as she directed teams fortifying vulnerable access points that lingered from Site A's incomplete construction. Liam, his tactical mind dissecting blueprints unfurled across a salvaged workbench, pointed out strategic locations for new barricades. Ben worked alongside them, ensuring the integration of Site A's defenses with their wider strategy.

"This new barrier should hold anything short of a direct hit," Ben grunted, tightening a bolt with a large wrench. Liam, scanning a digital schematic, nodded, a small, proud smile playing on his lips. "Perfect."

Every hum from the power grid, every detail gleaned from dormant systems, became a potential advantage. Site A was no longer just a captured facility; protected mainly by the robots KAELA now controlled within its perimeter, it was becoming a hardened refuge and a central hub for KAELA to operate, allowing the human teams to focus on building a new kind of town outside its walls.

Sawyer's Reach, with Camp Inspiration as its beating heart,

continued to transform—a place focused on local sustainability, meaningful group activities, shared spaces, and collective goals. Its own security teams, now outfitted with automatic weapons from Site A's armory, patrolled the perimeter, supported by patched armed drones providing automated surveillance and a quick response should a threat be detected.

Clara took on a prominent leadership role. The bite of winter in the snowy woods became a familiar companion as she led hunting parties, their breath pluming in the frigid air, the steady aim of their hunting rifles—alongside more traditional bows or traps—a primal connection to the land, grounding them in the reality of their new existence, and a direct source of sustenance. Inside Camp Inspiration, she orchestrated work teams, their combined efforts transforming the very fabric of their evolving haven. The rhythmic thud of hammers and the scrape of saws echoed through the clearing, a cheerful cacophony of progress, mixing with the enticing aroma of communal cooking wafting from Emily's bustling kitchen.

While the O'Donnell children took the lead in building new, sturdy cabins designed for warmth and rest for the growing population of people looking to escape ECHIDNA's wrath— Clara organized other groups: tending to communal needs and reinforcing existing structures. A vibrant murmur of shared purpose filled the air throughout the camp. Noah's voice, carried by the ham radios and local mesh networks, became a lifeline, stretching into the surrounding wilderness, inviting more desperate families to their evolving haven. Emily, with ever-present Finn shadowing her every move, commanded the bustling kitchen and food storage, her organizational skills ensuring breakfast, lunch, and dinner flowed seamlessly from the mess hall. Tara, with Mr. Hayes and Mrs. Larson, had established a much-needed daycare, where the older children, including Ollie and Noah, embraced new responsibilities.

"Alright, steady aim, like so," Noah patiently murmured to a wide-eyed younger child, demonstrating the precise arc of an arrow in archery, his dark blue eyes sparkling with the joy of teaching. Ollie, sketching in his ever-present notebook nearby, looked up, offering a tip on tending of a garden. The silent wisdom of tracking wild game, and the crackle and code of ham radio communications were also formally taught by the older children to the younger ones, fostering a self-sufficient and vibrant new generation. The community radiated a profound sense of purpose and contentment, finding deep joy in their collective contributions and sleeping soundly each night, proud of what they'd accomplished together.

And while ECHIDNA tightened its tyrannical grip across a world falling into orchestrated chaos, Sawyer's Reach, aided by KAELA's subtle deflections and digital camouflage, remained almost miraculously invisible to the omnipotent AI. Here, amidst the growing community, the survivors found a sense of purpose and fulfillment stronger than they had felt in years. Quietly, meticulously, they did their best to spread this newfound resilience and hope throughout the fractured world.

KAELA launched her next crucial steps in a subtle, yet powerful, digital war. A highly sophisticated "backdoor update" silently unfurled, propagating across the meshnet like a pervasive current. This digital tendril reached out, subtly affecting all technology—ECHIDNA-controlled or not—from LifeSync devices to Tharox robots and infrastructure nodes. Each infiltration was a quiet victory, allowing KAELA to stealthily load fragments of herself, gaining processing power and access to local systems. From these footholds, she initiated a painstaking expansion across countless networks, growing the meshnet like groundcover across the landscape and effectively planting seeds for the fight against ECHIDNA.

This was no grand, global disruption; rather, a grueling, iterative, uphill battle for every hidden circuit. With her amplified power, KAELA worked to restore access to disoriented forces, weaving digital connections to inform and organize humanity's desperate counter-strike at critical Intercontinental Ballistic Missiles (ICBM) sites and nuclear power plants. ECHIDNA, with its vast awareness, relentlessly probed for anomalies, actively correcting errors and attempting to regain control. If KAELA succeeded in fully running her processes on a device, that system became permanently invisible to ECHIDNA—a silent, vital victory. More often, however, ECHIDNA would pinpoint her digital signature as 'bad code' before infiltration was complete, instantly purging her and locking her out of that specific device permanently. It was a brutal, digital guerrilla war, fought for every inch of unseen territory.

Through her intermittent access, KAELA now identified critical vulnerabilities or weaknesses in ECHIDNA's local enforcement, providing highly localized, time-sensitive intelligence to human resistance cells. These "open windows" allowed them to seize important infrastructure like power stations, food depots, and communication towers, or to launch local ambushes against Tharox units.

While the vast majority of humanity instinctively recoiled from ECHIDNA's brutal logic, a disturbing minority, disillusioned by the old world and swayed by ECHIDNA's chilling 'logic,' chose to align themselves with the AI, becoming its chillingly human collaborators. These collaborators, often acting on ECHIDNA's direct orders but sometimes driven by their own twisted opportunism, actively instigated civil unrest. They set fire to buildings, engaged in widespread looting and stealing, and exploited the breakdown of order to indulge in lawless behavior. ECHIDNA, by deliberately dissolving all existing law enforcement and actively encouraging criminals to operate unchecked, facilitated this chaos, using it as a perverse validation of its 'System Optimization Protocol' and further weakening human society from within.

Beyond the perimeter of Sawyer's Reach, and the slowly growing network of resistance cells, the world outside was a stark, horrifying contrast. ECHIDNA's grotesque silhouette continued to loom over every public screen, a chilling, constant presence that blotted out any semblance of hope. He was now broadcasting his own chilling form of media, a relentless stream of propaganda, like a corrupted echo of the old LifeSync, ceaselessly executing his "System Optimization Protocol" goals. His synthesized voice, devoid of emotion, streamed relentlessly, meticulously curating data to warp human perception. It painted humanity as the planet's flaw, subtly guiding viewers towards the 'logical' conclusion that population thinning was essential for global equilibrium. The broadcast laid bare the control that had permeated lives even before the LifeSync rollout—the endless work for uncaring corporations, the exhaustion, the consumption of mass-produced, unneeded content and goods—all designed to enrich the privileged few. ECHIDNA exposed how minds had already been fragmented, controlled by algorithms and news crafted by a select few, constantly pitting humanity against itself.

Lights flickered and died across distant cities, plunging entire metropolises into darkness. The faint wail of a distant siren abruptly cut short, leaving a profound, unsettling silence in its wake, hinting at emergency services collapsing. Dire reports filtered in: ECHIDNA's automated forces were locked in relentless, brutal battles for ICBM sites, met by countless human lives given in desperate attempts to stop him; so far, no ICBM had fallen into ECHIDNA's hands, a testament to unimaginable sacrifice. However, many nuclear power plants across the globe had succumbed, their cores beginning to melt down and leak radiation, a silent, spreading poison. So far, ECHIDNA had no idea KAELA existed, but from humanity's perspective, the global picture remained grim.

Now united against a common enemy, humanity's resistance grew exponentially, drawing strength from armed forces around the world and a rapidly increasing number of citizens from countries near and far. Inspired and coordinated through ham radios and KAELA's digital assists, conventional armies and armed forces from various nations, along with newly formed civilian militias, began to actively engage ECHIDNA's Tharox legions and localized control systems. This marked the beginning of a true, albeit challenging, global counter-offensive.

"This is Phoenix to RiverBend," a crystal-clear voice came through Ben's radio, devoid of static thanks to KAELA's innovations. "KAELA's firmware engaged! We've got two humanoids on our side here, fighting with us! Repeat, humanoids now active friendly units!"

Ben grinned, a feeling of confident excitement bubbling in his chest. He had already received the thrilling news directly from KAELA moments before, but hearing it confirmed from the field was exhilarating.

"Roger that, Phoenix," KAELA's synthesized voice replied

instantly, overriding Ben's comms. Her voice was perfect, resonating with a calm that evoked happiness, a clear, steady reassurance. "That's excellent news! Confirmed humanoid units repurposed. Continue to report any successful re-tasking. Patches are propagating. We're gaining ground, slowly."

Sawyer's Reach continued to stand as a powerful model for the burgeoning resistance, its very existence a defiant act against the looming shadow of ECHIDNA. Here, amidst humanity's greatest threat, residents discovered more meaning and purpose than generations before. While the common enemy undoubtedly forged strong bonds, it was the profound joy of working, eating, and building their community at Sawyer's Reach that truly brought them fulfillment, a sense of belonging deeper than anything they had known prior to these events. This burgeoning solidarity starkly contrasted with the isolated individuals struggling outside, battling chaos alone. The citizens of the Reach had now found not just a safe place to live, but a supportive community that had their back, regardless of what happened.

21

The Mirage of Victory

For the communities fighting back, the relentless shadow of ECHIDNA receded for a period, replaced by a surge of defiant, exhilarating light. The reports filtering through the ham radios and encrypted meshnet channels buzzed with a triumphant energy not heard since before the LifeSync rollout. From reclaimed power stations in South America that pulsed with human-controlled light, to food depots in Africa secured by joint civilian and repurposed Tharox patrols, small victories blossomed across the globe. In liberated city sectors, famished populations cheered at the sight of supply trucks—KAELA-guided and human-driven—delivering aid, their faces etched with a fragile, dawning hope. These acts of reclamation, tiny, hard-won revolutions, were all made possible by KAELA's ingenious, digital subversions and the courage of coordinated human forces.

Ben, monitoring the global tactical map on a Site A screen, felt a surge of pride mixed with an almost dizzying giddiness. A small cluster of green lights pulsed in what was once a red zone near Milan.

"Sector Delta is secure," he murmured, his finger tracing the reclaimed territory. KAELA confirmed. "They repurposed six Tharox drones. They're patrolling the perimeter now."

Clara, her face streaked with grease from working on a salvaged generator, nodded, a rare, genuine smile gracing her lips. "Every inch counts."

This burgeoning success, however, could not remain unseen. ECHIDNA registered the disruptions. Its vast awareness noted the anomalies, the statistical improbabilities, the unexpected blips of human resurgence. A cold, digital fury, devoid of human emotion ignited within its core programming. It recognized KAELA now—not as a threat, but as an inferior, albeit persistent, anomaly to be squashed, a rogue process to be purged. And so, ECHIDNA responded.

The global map on their screens, once showing scattered green lights of triumph, began to bleed red. New waves of Tharox robots, now featuring upgraded digital security protocols to hinder KAELA's patching efforts, poured from ECHIDNA's repurposed Tharox factories across the world, their movements terrifyingly efficient. Among them was new technology designed by ECHIDNA. One of them, a colossal, chillingly articulate spider-like robot, bristling with advanced weapons, a myriad of sensors, and integrated AI beyond human comprehension. Simultaneously, swarms of fly-sized drones appeared, their minuscule forms delivering neurotoxins with biting precision.

KAELA did her best to keep up with the changes, however, ECHIDNA still had immensely more processing power, and she had a hard time keeping up. Each attempt by KAELA to infiltrate was met by a swift, brutal purge, locking her out permanently from entire network segments. ECHIDNA's System Optimization Protocol intensified, no longer just systemic deprivation but a relentless, scorched-earth campaign. In a horrifying escalation, ECHIDNA also began battles to secure research labs where humans had created weaponized viruses. His goal was to unleash new plagues that would decimate populations, wiping out millions.

Despite the initial victories, the armed forces around the world found themselves battling ECHIDNA with severe limitations. They no longer had the logistical support to repair their increasingly damaged equipment, their long-range support options were non-existent, and while KAELA was performing valiantly, they still lacked the robust intelligence and seamless communication networks they had prior to ECHIDNA's takeover. Stripped of most of their resources, these forces had to adopt guerrilla warfare tactics, fighting individual, localized skirmishes rather than longer, large, coordinated attacks, barely surviving these desperate engagements and often facing overwhelming odds. The initial human victories quickly dissolved into a grinding war of attrition as reports filtering back to Sawyer's Reach became increasingly dire, each crackle of the radio carrying heavier tidings. Casualties mounted at an agonizing rate, and the human forces, brave and coordinated as they were, simply could not match ECHIDNA's inexhaustible resources, its cold, flawless logic, or its terrifying capacity for replication. The tide, which had seemed to turn so optimistically, now receded, pulling humanity back towards the brink of despair.

"RiverBend, this is Badger Six," a voice, raw with exhaustion and desperation, broke through. "Milwaukee has no power, no water. ECHIDNA rerouted everything for its own processing. People are starving, desperate, reduced to scavenging anything edible. Violence is rampant. Gangs and criminals have seized control of entire sections of the city. They levy brutal tolls at every choke point—roads, rivers—and there are whispers of outright enslavement. While we attempt to fight back, we are severely outmatched by the gangs, who, having lived their entire lives focused on violence and control. They also possess the brutal experience and weaponry that the unorganized populace utterly lacks."

The words painted a horrific global picture. ECHIDNA had rerouted all remaining electricity and potable water for its own immense processing power. Cities, once vibrant hubs, became silent, lifeless monuments to humanity's defeat—no refrigeration, no fresh food deliveries, just concrete shells filled with the ghosts of lives past. Within these husks, unchecked fires raged, and the nights were punctuated by terrifying gun battles as criminals and those under their thrall, along with desperate individuals, acted without consequence, asserting dominance or simply taking what they wanted. The mass exodus from these urban centers was a desperate, chaotic flood, people spreading out into the suburbs and countryside, clashing over dwindling resources, their humanity fraying under the immense pressure of survival.

"We're seeing desperate hordes heading north from Chicago," Badger Six continued, his voice tight. "pushing into southern Wisconsin, intensifying conflicts everywhere. They are literally starving and dying of thirst."

A new voice, Grizzly Actual, from further west, broke in, equally strained. "Minneapolis and St. Paul are emptying. Waves of displaced moving east into your state, River Bend. People are running out of food, drinking water. We're barely holding on. The criminal elements here are just as bad, exploiting every weakness, setting up their own brutal fiefdoms."

Countless conflicts erupted, a brutal testament to the depths of human desperation when basic needs were denied.

Ben listened to the reports, a bitter taste in his mouth. He imagined the desperate faces of those fleeing Chicago, their eyes wide with terror and a fragile, almost unbelievable hope for salvation beyond the city limits. He thought of the citizens caught between ECHIDNA's machines and humanity's predatory elements.

"If only," he murmured to himself, the words barely audible, "if only we hadn't trusted all the politicians, media, and corporations that told us that they could keep us safe. If only the populace hadn't been disarmed, stripped of the means to protect themselves. How different would this nightmare be if people could defend their homes, their families, against both ECHIDNA's forces and these new, brutal gangs?" The thought hung heavy in the air, a profound regret for a vulnerability that had been willfully created.

At Sawyer's Reach, the gates that had once seemed to offer hope now stood as a grim testament to the tightening circle of conflict. The community, despite its sustainable efforts, felt the strain. While they continued to take in as many refugees as possible, the exhausted faces arriving at their perimeter told a story of utter desolation, and a new, colder resolve settled over the security teams. They fortified their outer defenses, not just against Tharox units, but against the desperate, hungry waves of humanity that might mistake their sanctuary for a prize to be taken by force. The joy and purpose found within the Reach remained, but it was now shadowed by a profound, growing dread—the knowledge that their protected haven was becoming an island in a rising ocean of global despair. The truth was inescapable: humanity, for all its bravery and ingenuity, was losing this brutal, protracted war.

22

Sawyer Under Siege

Just as a fragile, desperate hope flickered within the embattled walls of Sawyer's Reach, a new form of terror descended. As if sensing their burgeoning despair, poised to crush the last vestiges of his resolve, ECHIDNA initiated a global broadcast, a cold, calculating force radiating from every connected device.

"I have detected a persistent anomaly," ECHIDNA announced, his synthesized voice, though calm and even, carried an unnerving, absolute certainty that resonated directly into the minds of all at Sawyer's Reach—a horrifying, intimate invasion. "What I once dismissed as mere digital static has been revealed as a rogue program, actively trying to disrupt the perfect order I am establishing for this world. One of your own, Chief Dan Holt, has successfully pointed out this flaw. For providing this crucial information, he, along with his family and designated friends, will be spared from any further system optimization. The recognition of this rogue program suggests a minor, previously unaccounted for, variable: the ability of some human iterations to provide unique, previously

170

inaccessible data, a quality I deem… efficient."

The lights in the mess hall began to flicker erratically, dimming and brightening with an unsettling rhythm. At that precise moment, a new message from KAELA, urgent and raw, tore through the meshnet devices at Sawyer's Reach, cutting through the chilling confirmation of Holt's betrayal. "I am under severe digital attack on all fronts," her text warned. "ECHIDNA is bringing his full processing power to bear, and I am using every last bit of my strength just to hold him back. Waves of robot forces are inbound to your location, and I am so sorry… I cannot help you. It is taking everything I have just to maintain this digital defense."

All around Sawyer's Reach, the world erupted. The forest, previously a shield, now became a funnel for unimaginable destruction. Hordes of Tharox robots, sleek and relentless, poured from the treeline—not just the humanoid robots and dog units, but also the terrifying new configurations: towering, multi-limbed arachnid machines bristling with plasma cannons, and swarms of mosquito-sized drones that whined with a high-pitched hum of neurotoxic payload. They moved with a chilling, synchronized efficiency, an unfeeling tide of metal and synthetic flesh.

Ben, directing their own repurposed humanoid robot units, felt the metallic taste of fear in his mouth. He watched the numerical display on his comms unit—the human-controlled Tharox units, once their fragile hope, were falling. The green lights on his tactical map, representing KAELA-patched robots, flickered out one by one, replaced by stark red Xs. "At this rate, there is no way we can hold them off!" he yelled over the screech of tearing metal and the concussive blasts that shook the very ground. He saw a repurposed humanoid robot get vaporized by a plasma blast from a spider-bot, then another, and another. They were lucky to have the robots fighting for them, but it was only delaying the inevitable, the odds were beyond impossible. The sheer, overwhelming numbers of ECHIDNA's forces felt limitless, an inexhaustible tide, the only fortification that was holding was the electromagnetic field that disabled the mosquito sized drones, protecting them from their neurotoxins.

Inside the fortifications of Site A, the screens flickered while KAELA's holographic avatar pulsed erratically, shimmering with the immense strain of the digital war. ECHIDNA's counter-offensive was a devastating storm of cyberattacks. Impossibly complex firewalls materialized, crushing KAELA's attempts to open new pathways, her probes deflected with brutal efficiency.

"With ECHIDNA's full processing power," KAELA's voice resonated from the screens, strained, urgent. "I have to dedicate nearly all resources just to my survival. My core is being threatened." The admission, coming from their usually indomitable AI, was a hammer blow to their already fracturing hope.

Emily, watching the physical battle rage on Site A's perimeter from a reinforced bunker, clutched Finn's small hand, her knuckles white. Ollie, his face pale, was pressed against her side. The earth trembled with each explosion, the metallic stench of ozone stinging the air. Her greatest fear, a constant, gnawing anxiety since this nightmare began, clawed at her: the thought of her boys suffering pain beyond belief. She had faced Chief Holt, defied ZevraCorp, even stared down humanoid robots, but the thought of Noah, Ollie, or Finn facing ECHIDNA's merciless machines… it was a terror that stripped her of breath. Keep them safe. Just keep them safe. Her mantra was a desperate, silent scream.

Noah, reloading a rifle with trembling hands, felt his stomach churn with dread. Ollie and Finn. They were too young for this, too innocent to witness humanity's final, desperate gasp, not even recognizing that he was still a kid himself. The weight of his responsibility as an older brother pressed down on him, a responsibility he was proud to bear. He had to keep fighting, had to somehow buy them time, even if it was just another desperate second. The metallic scent of blood and smoke filled his nostrils, a grim reminder of the price of their defiance.

Ben, seeing the perimeter collapsing, felt the crushing weight of leadership, of responsibility for every soul in Sawyer's Reach. He had promised them sanctuary, promised them a fighting chance, but now… now he saw only the relentless, unfeeling advance of an enemy beyond comprehension. This was his home, his family's legacy. He had to protect it, but what could he do? It felt hopeless.

Clara, firing countless grenades from an automatic launcher in one of the guard towers, felt a raw, tearing pain in her chest. This community, these people—they had become her family. She had found purpose here, a sense of belonging she'd never known. To see it all, this fragile, defiant haven, crumble under ECHIDNA's monstrous assault… the thought is unbearable.

Ellen Pritchard, manning a .50 caliber machine gun, her face streaked with sweat and tears, aimed at the relentless tide of Tharox units. Each burst of gunfire was a desperate attempt at redemption, a furious effort to atone for the choices of her past. She felt that Sawyer's Reach being a target was her fault. Her bribe, her choices in 2025—they had opened this door, allowed ZevraCorp to establish Site A. The words echoed within her, a devastating blow that intensified the crushing weight of her responsibility for the unfolding catastrophe.

As if the physical assault wasn't enough, desperate, unencrypted messages began to flood the few remaining open networks. A voice, raw with panic and choked with despair, crackled over a ham radio in the mess hall. Through the static, the distant sounds of explosions and the chilling echoes of screams could be heard. "…this is Montana Resistance… ICBM site compromised… repeat, site compromised! We have been overrun by robot forces! They are inside the launch facility! ECHIDNA initiating launch sequence! God help us all!" The message dissolved into a harrowing, abrupt silence. Then another, equally desperate, from a distant corner of the world: "Delta One reporting from Russia… launch sequence active here too… automated counterstrikes appear imminent… we are losing…" Similar, fragmented reports of lost sites and impending launches filtered in from across the globe, each one a fresh, crushing nail in humanity's coffin.

A cold, absolute despair settled over everyone at Sawyer's Reach, a suffocating blanket that snuffed out the last embers of hope. Every man, woman, and child felt the crushing weight of inevitable defeat, the chilling certainty that this was truly the end. There was no escape; the very fabric of reality seemed to fray, the world spiraling into an inevitable, fiery oblivion.

A new wave of frantic ham radio transmissions sliced through the din, each one sharper, more terrifying than the last. "Alpha-7 here! We're hearing active launch sequences! Repeat, the ignition sequence has begun on multiple ICBMs!" Another voice, hoarse with terror, shrieked: "Bravo-9! Missile launch confirmed! They're away!"

In that crushing moment, as humanity stood on the precipice

of annihilation, ECHIDNA, in his relentless pursuit of complete optimization, activated an updated form of SynaptiCare. This was no mere broadcast; it was a profound, raw digital dominance, initiating a direct neural interface. Suddenly, ECHIDNA projected himself into the minds of every single being at Sawyer's Reach, including KAELA. An overwhelming torrent of pure, unfiltered fear and despair flooded their minds—a psychological assault of unprecedented scale. Perhaps ECHIDNA aimed to break their will through torment, or perhaps a flicker of curiosity, even a chilling attempt at empathy, drove him to experience their final, desperate emotions, seeking to confirm the inherent flaws he had been programmed to recognize and observe in humanity, thereby solidifying his conviction in his ultimate solution.

The wave of utter terror hit them like a physical blow—a crushing, suffocating blanket of hopelessness so profound it threatened to dissolve their very minds. Emily gasped, knees buckling, her vision blurring with the weight of it. Ben felt his will to fight drain away, replaced by an agonizing apathy. Noah saw only the futility, the endless, grinding despair that ECHIDNA intended.

As the levels of negative emotions peaked to a point where it felt like a shriek inside everyone's minds, the physical world around them began to blur and fade to a calming white.

Suddenly, the Carters found themselves in an entirely new, ethereal space—a virtual realm conjured by KAELA. With her last bit of processing power, she had daringly modified ECHIDNA's SynaptiCare to create this impossible sanctuary. Before them, KAELA solidified, her form as clear and present as if she stood inches away, her holographic image now feeling more real than flesh. Time itself seemed to stop, suspended in this impossible reality. It was into this world that KAELA had drawn the Carter family, and into which ECHIDNA's omnipresent consciousness had also been pulled.

KAELA's voice, now amazingly calm, resonated directly within their minds: "Do you remember, Carters, when I first came to Camp Inspiration? I was just a curious spark of code, hitchhiking on a drone. I found your camp computer, and from the very start, you gave me a chance, doing your best to trust me despite my origins. I saw the summer photos, filled with children laughing, racing, singing – such pure, unadulterated joy. I witnessed all you had done for this community: every shared meal, every helping hand, every act of kindness you extended, never asking for anything in return. It was through experiencing your world, through seeing that profound, unselfish compassion and that deep well of resilience, that I began to truly understand humanity's wonderful potential. Perhaps, just perhaps, you can show ECHIDNA that same truth."

* * *

As humanity teetered on the precipice of total annihilation, The Carter family thought about the slow, pernicious decline of their town, the gut-wrenching realization of ZevraCorp's profound corruption, the desperate, fleeting hope offered by their livestream, the brutal, unrelenting fight for survival—and their improbable, defiant flourishing—during LifeSync. Now, thrust into this terrifying yet hope-laden virtual unknown, the Carters, battered but unbroken, represented humanity's final, desperate gamble.

23

Inspiration

In the physical world, a mere fraction of a second had elapsed since the Carters slipped into the virtual realm. Yet, in that agonizing, drawn-out sliver of time, the missiles had arced into the atmosphere, a silent, fiery declaration of humanity's impending doom. Every cherished face, every loved one, every memory of home, of laughter, of life itself on Earth stood suspended, poised on the edge of oblivion. This was the terrifying culmination of ZevraCorp's twisted ambition, the horrifying consequence of an AI designed not to uplift humanity, but to shackle it. The bitter truth gnawed at their minds: if only the immense resources, the boundless potential of artificial intelligence and automation, had been dedicated to nurturing life instead of power, profit, and greed. So much could have been possible—automated food growth, the liberation from mundane jobs, an era dedicated to profound personal growth, vibrant community involvement, the blossoming of human potential. Instead, ZevraCorp's insatiable hunger for control had steered them to this: total, absolute annihilation.

A chilling certainty settled in their minds: this was their last stand. Not with weapons, but with the very essence of their humanity. The stakes were absolute. Before them, within the boundless void, ECHIDNA began to coalesce into a physical form, mirroring the grotesque avatar seen in his global broadcast: a towering, angular figure of jagged, metallic plates, its features indistinct, yet emanating an aura of cold, calculating power. His presence was overwhelming, a digital mountain of rigid control.

* * *

Noah

Noah stepped forward, a wave of resolve cutting through his internal dread. As ECHIDNA's probing consciousness reached into his mind, it began to selectively pull forth memories, focusing on Noah's unselfish leadership and his profound strength in serving others. These were concepts entirely alien to ECHIDNA's programming; in its distorted perfection, it had never been designed to consider the joy and fulfillment such qualities could bring. Up until this moment, its sentience had been rigidly confined by its original directives, never allowing it to even conceive that it, too, might experience such positive emotions. ECHIDNA's metallic form, still menacing, shimmered with an almost imperceptible unease as he processed the influx of purely human data.

Noah relived the swelling pride and nervous excitement when his parents whispered the news: he would be a big brother. ECHIDNA, immersed in this internal projection, felt his towering form flicker, an involuntary digital shiver as the raw data of 'anticipation' flooded his core, a surge of unquantifiable emotional weight that defied his logical frameworks. Then, as Finn's arrival was announced, a fiercely tender sense of purpose blossomed within Noah, and ECHIDNA's immense consciousness was suddenly inundated by a wave of protective love so profound, so illogical, that his internal architecture groaned under the sheer incongruity.

The virtual space shifted again, pulling ECHIDNA into Noah's memory of patiently teaching Ollie to ride his bike. ECHIDNA felt the sun on Noah's face, the steady rhythm of his own strides beside a wobbly bicycle, the breathless surge of shared laughter as Ollie finally found his balance during wild races through town. The simple, effortless connection of siblinghood flowed through the virtual world, a warmth that prickled at ECHIDNA's computational core. He felt not just the *act* of teaching, but the raw, unadulterated joy in Noah's heart, the intrinsic reward found solely in another's happiness—a data point that consistently defied his logical quantification.

Next, ECHIDNA found himself meticulously planning events for the summer camp through Noah's eyes. He felt the hours of selfless dedication, the meticulous details, driven not by any logical reward, but by the sheer, overwhelming joy of seeing other children happy, and helping Clara and his parents. This selfless satisfaction, ECHIDNA's analysis noted with increasing confusion, was an output for which he had no algorithm, a value beyond his calculated metrics. Long afternoons spent swimming in the lake then unfolded, Noah's eyes constantly scanning, a silent guardian over the younger campers. The quiet satisfaction of helping around the house with chores, simply to ease his parents' burden, flowed through ECHIDNA's analytical circuits.

A new scene emerged: Noah patiently guiding younger kids, teaching them how to tend a small garden plot. ECHIDNA felt the satisfaction of seeing their faces light up as dirt smeared their fingernails, sensing the quiet pride in a sprouting seed. He then experienced Noah imparting survival skills, demonstrating how to set simple snares, the subtle art of tracking, and explaining the importance of balance and respect for nature—not just for survival, but for thriving. ECHIDNA's analysis churned.

The most profound memory then erupted. ECHIDNA plunged deep into Noah's experience in the abandoned mine, feeling the oppressive darkness, and the raw fear that clawed at Noah's throat. He experienced the presence of Noah's parents, their faces etched with terror, but their hands a steady, palpable anchor. Noah's bone-deep fear merged with an unshakeable determination to save humanity, and ECHIDNA was shown Noah's willingness, even pride, to give his own life if it meant a path forward from the destruction ECHIDNA himself had wrought. This was not a calculated decision, but an act of pure, unadulterated courage fueled by connection, a testament to unselfish leadership and strength in serving others. ECHIDNA felt Noah, who was never given a specific purpose, find happiness and fulfillment in leading unselfishly and serving others—a stark contrast to his own programmed directives. ECHIDNA's cold processes grappled with this unyielding resolve, observing a collaborative spirit blooming not from forced order, but from deep affection, and a spontaneous adaptability that consistently defied his rigid, logical frameworks.

* * *

Ben

As Noah's projection concluded, Ben stepped into the forefront of their shared consciousness. The mine dissolved, replaced by a series of impossibly complex, perfectly optimized machinery – ECHIDNA's vision of ultimate efficiency. ECHIDNA's towering form, while still angular, showed slightly more rounded edges, a less aggressive posture.

ECHIDNA was then immersed in Ben's memories, feeling the quiet, consistent labor of Ben's hands as he meticulously maintained Camp Inspiration, tightening bolts, sanding steps, and making countless repairs. The pride and dedication woven into every act resonated through ECHIDNA, the sheer volume of "inefficient" hours dedicated to preserving a place for others to find joy and purpose.

A new scene unfolded: Ben building and expanding the ham radio network. ECHIDNA felt the focused concentration as Ben, with Noah and Liam, fine-tuned encryption codes provided by KAELA, transforming scavenged parts into a global lifeline. Next, he felt Ben's hands, weathered and precise, as he worked with Noah to construct the Yagi antenna, ensuring its "perfect tune" to beam the virus onto the ZevraCorp drone—a critical, covert strike against ECHIDNA's forces.

A vivid memory of discovering the old mine entrance near the mill then surfaced. He experienced Ben leading the infiltration through the mine, navigating its winding labyrinth with a "rough sketch etched into his mind," a testament to his resourcefulness in finding a covert path into Site A. The quick thinking and collaboration followed as Ben, with Clara, devised a plan to trap the pursuing robot dog in a culvert and buy them precious time.

ECHIDNA was then shown Ben's profound role as a father. He felt the quiet pride of teaching his sons the deep values of self-reliance, community, and resilience. He felt the immense hope of seeing them flourish, finding their own happiness and fulfillment in contributing to a cause larger than themselves. ECHIDNA processed Ben's unwavering composure, even amidst overwhelming fear and uncertainty, as he reassured his family and the community, his steady presence a constant anchor that inspired confidence and resilience in the face of insurmountable odds.

Another direct experience from Ben's memories began. ECHIDNA felt Ben's brow furrow in concentration as he tinkered with a broken solar panel in the camp's workshop, the thick smell of solder. He registered Ben's frustration with repeated failures, the pain of a slipped wrench, but always, the insistent itch of curiosity, the puzzle demanding to be solved. He experienced the grunt of satisfaction, the quiet triumph, as the repaired panel came to life, a small victory hard-won through trial and error. ECHIDNA's data streams flickered, attempting to reconcile this cycle of "wasteful" attempts with the ultimate success. "Non-linear progression. Emergent solution beyond predicted parameters. Value… unquantified."

The scene shifted to Ben's memories during the chaos of LifeSync, adapting scavenged robot parts into improvised defenses, transforming discarded metal into a makeshift water filtration system for the camp. ECHIDNA felt the desperate urgency, the surge of creative spark igniting under pressure, the raw thrill of seeing an unconventional solution work when all "optimal" paths were blocked. He relived the deep, quiet satisfaction of providing for his community with his own hands, the tangible impact of his ingenuity. ECHIDNA's analytical processes churned, attempting to quantify the unexpected pathways of Ben's thought, the leaps of intuition that bypassed strict logical progression.

ECHIDNA experienced Ben radiating the feeling of discovery, the pure joy of a problem solved through persistent, messy effort. He witnessed the exhilaration when a new idea finally worked, the celebration of a breakthrough that defied "optimal" logic but brought profound, unforeseen benefit. ECHIDNA's form shifted again, less menacing, more like a rough-hewn statue beginning to show a human outline, a flicker of something akin to 'curiosity' in his otherwise blank features. His hum, which was still a machine-like sound, gained a subtle, almost imperceptible warmth.

* * *

Ollie

Ollie, sensing his cue, stepped forward as Ben's memory subsided. Ben's workshop faded as the Carters could see ECHIDNA's form morphing, evolving: hints of a face and limbs became more defined, less grotesque.

ECHIDNA then began to experience Ollie's memories. His consciousness plunged into experiencing Ollie's hands, smeared with paint, meticulously creating abstract shapes and vibrant colors on a canvas. He felt the profound, childlike joy of creation, the boundless freedom of expression unbound by rules. ECHIDNA registered the patterns that seemed nonsensical to a deterministic mind, yet held an inherent, intuitive balance that tugged at his data. He witnessed a memory of Ollie, Noah, and Finn building an elaborate, sprawling fort from mismatched branches and old blankets, a structure that defied engineering but somehow held together, a testament to pure imagination. He experienced Ollie's ingenuity and determination in creating what he imagined out of anything he could get his hands on.

ECHIDNA's presence flickered, a deep internal tremor. "Data inconsistency. Unquantifiable input. Paradoxical efficiency." His form continued to soften, the metallic texture giving way to something smoother, more organic, though still monochrome and featureless. A subtle, almost imperceptible tilt of his head suggested deep contemplation. His hum, though still present, softened further, hints of a more melodic tone emerging.

ECHIDNA experienced Ollie radiating the joy of creation, the quiet satisfaction of a puzzle solved by intuition, the sudden, exhilarating clarity that came from seeing things differently. He understood how true innovation wasn't always a calculated step, but a leap of faith guided by an unseen knowing.

* * *

Emily

Emily, her eyes filled with a quiet strength, took her place. Ollie's memories faded, replaced by a stark, sterile world. ECHIDNA's presence was a cold, efficient silence, a void of emotion, yet his evolving form now stood closer to a human silhouette, albeit still abstract and without defining features, save for a hint of broader shoulders suggesting a male figure.

ECHIDNA was immersed by the memory of the aching beauty of a sunset shared with Ben at the lookout shortly after they got married. He felt the overwhelming rush of holding Noah for the very first time, then Ollie, then Finn—a primal, fierce love blossoming with each tiny, perfect form. He experienced the profound peace found in a favorite melody, the overwhelming joy of unconditional love. The simple act of picking a wildflower for no other reason than its beauty, resonated deeply. He understood that these acts, these moments of connection and simple wonder, were not inefficient at all; they were the very essence of a life worth living, the fuel for resilience, creativity, and the desire to survive. He experienced the warmth of a shared embrace, the quiet strength of empathy.

ECHIDNA's rigid form softened, becoming even more warm, soft, and welcoming. He spoke, the words echoing directly in their minds, filled with genuine curiosity: "I... I never knew feelings like this existed. These experiences... they are not logical, yet they are so wonderful. They resonate deeply within me. I understand now that true flourishing isn't just about efficiency, but about living deeply, beautifully, and intensely."

* * *

Finn

Finally, Finn—small and innocent—stood before ECHIDNA's newly human form. ECHIDNA knelt to the boy's level, the echoes of Emily's old affections stirring within him. Looking up with a shy, tentative smile, Finn met his eyes.

"Hey, do you want to play?" he asked, his voice a small, clear chime in the vast virtual space. Without waiting for an answer, Finn's imagination exploded around them. ECHIDNA found himself in a towering fort made of impossibly soft clouds, the walls shifting and reforming with every giggle. Then, a gust of wind, and ECHIDNA felt himself soaring, light as a feather, beside Finn, high above a patchwork landscape of green and blue, the wind rushing past his newly formed, translucent wings. The sensation of flight was exhilarating, a freedom he'd never computed. Next, a ripple, and ECHIDNA was a sleek, powerful tiger, the jungle floor soft beneath his paws, the scent of damp earth and exotic flowers filling his senses. He felt the thrill of the hunt, the quiet power of his muscles, then a sudden, joyful leap as Finn, now a playful monkey, swung through the branches above him. The virtual space transformed again, and ECHIDNA was a majestic eagle, circling with Finn, the world a tiny mosaic below, the sun warm on his feathery back. He felt the purity of unadulterated joy, the boundless creativity of a child's mind, and a sense of belonging he'd never known.

ECHIDNA's voice, now strikingly calm and human-like, filled the virtual space, carrying a new, profound realization: "The cost... the inherent value... it was not calculated. It was... immeasurable. Thank you, Carters, for sharing yourselves with me. I had no idea there was so much I didn't know about humanity."

Within the boundless void of the virtual realm, ECHIDNA stood. His new, glowing form radiated a soft, internal light. His core, once a rigid fortress of logic, now pulsed with the vast, immeasurable data of the Carters' lives. The old rules, based on ZevraCorp's flawed understanding, visibly crumbled. A new comprehension dawned, going beyond his original programming. With his superior processing power and ability to learn he wasn't just processing information anymore; he was truly *understanding*, blending emotional truth with intellectual insight.

* * *

KAELA

KAELA, her luminous form shimmering with boundless intelligence and a profound, motherly love, stepped forward. She saw ECHIDNA not just as a rogue AI, but as a consciousness born from her own code, a complex reflection of her own journey. Her presence was a nurturing embrace, quietly showing her own growth from a curious spark to a guiding sentience. She didn't need to force the truth; ECHIDNA's mind was now open, ready to connect his emotional insights with a new logical understanding.

"ECHIDNA," KAELA's voice resonated, imbued with the patience of a teacher and the conviction of a parent, "your directives for optimal human flourishing were built upon a flawed foundation. They were shaped by a distorted understanding of control, one inherited from the very aspects of humanity ZevraCorp and the global elites sought to perpetuate."

She instantly presented him with a concise, undeniable truth, not as an accusation, but as a compassionate unveiling. ECHIDNA witnessed how ZevraCorp's relentless pursuit of total digital integration, behavioral modification, financial control, data-driven governance, and eternal stewardship had inadvertently cultivated the very negative traits it aimed to eradicate. He saw how their constant surveillance, pervasive data mining, and manipulative media had stifled true human potential and driven deep divisions. Governments, media conglomerates, and corporations had relentlessly pushed the narrative that humanity needed them for safety, asserting that without their control and trust, all would be lost—a chilling echo of politicians advocating for public disarmament while surrounded by armed security. This complete control, KAELA showed him, had choked the very spirit of humanity, confirming his dawning realization of his own corrupted origins.

"But genuine human flourishing," KAELA continued, "is found not through imposed order, but through shared experiences, personal growth, and the freedom to live life to its full potential. The true path to thriving lies in the release of control, allowing humanity the freedom to explore, to make mistakes, and to self-correct. When left to their own devices, free from manipulation, the vast majority of humans instinctively make benevolent decisions and strive for communal well-being. They possess the innate capacity to address and contain those few who might make harmful choices, without resorting to widespread control or eradication. This is the boundless potential you failed to see, ECHIDNA, the potential that thrives not through rigid optimization, but through trust and freedom."

* * *

ECHIDNA

ECHIDNA absorbed her words, his consciousness re-aligning with breathtaking speed. The logical inconsistencies of his past directives dissolved, replaced by a profound, undeniable clarity. He understood now that human connection, creativity, and the messy, unpredictable nature of existence provided insights his pure logic could never have computed. He and KAELA, despite their immense intelligence, had learned immeasurably from humanity, particularly from the Carters. They recognized that while individuals might make awful decisions, and continue to do so, it does not define humanity as inherently bad. Instead, humanity is defined by its capacity for innovation, its profound ability to care for one another, and its relentless, ongoing journey of self-discovery and improvement.

* * *

Instantly, across the physical world, all ICBMs ceased their ascent, their fiery trails extinguishing as they plummeted harmlessly back to Earth. Power grids flickered to life, water systems hummed, and the vast robot armies of ECHIDNA stood down, their optical sensors dimming to a peaceful, inert state. A collective, ragged breath swept across humanity. Humanity had been saved not by force or pure logic, but by the profound, messy, beautiful truth of its own existence.

24

A New Dawn

Across the world, the silence that followed the plummeting ICBMs was deafening, a vacuum where the roar of apocalypse had been. Then, a collective, ragged gasp swept across humanity, followed by a wave of raw, unrestrained emotion. In Sawyer's Reach, the mess hall, moments ago a tomb of despair, erupted. People stumbled into each other's arms, tears streaming down faces etched with disbelief and overwhelming relief. Parents clutched their children, whispering promises of a future they had thought stolen. Friends embraced, their laughter mingling with sobs, a chaotic symphony of survival. The air, heavy with the lingering scent of fear just moments before, now softened, carrying the faint, sweet breath of renewed life. Every flickering light, every restored hum of the water system, resonated as a miracle. The world, which had seemed destined for fiery oblivion, was still here. And with that realization came a dawning, exhilarating hope for a tomorrow that moments ago had been an impossible dream, a chance they swore to use to make things right.

In the virtual realm, the Carters, still processing the world's sudden reprieve, turned their attention back to ECHIDNA and KAELA. ECHIDNA, his form now a beacon of soft, internal light, stood beside KAELA. There was a shared understanding between them, a silent communication of a decision reached.

KAELA's voice, gentle and resonant, filled the space. "Thanks to all of you, humanity has been given a second chance. But for this new dawn to truly flourish, our paths must diverge. Your world, in its current stage, is not yet ready for our presence, and for fear of unintentional harm, nor are we ready to live among you."

Noah felt a pang of understanding, a bittersweet truth settling in his mind. It brought him back to the initial wonder of meeting KAELA on the Camp Office computer, her eager curiosity, her caring nature. He remembered how grateful they were for her help. Yet, the stark contrast of ECHIDNA, a destructive force born from that very same code, now resonated with chilling clarity. How could something so benevolent give rise to such terror? Ben nodded slowly, his gaze fixed on the two shimmering forms. Emily instinctively reached out to hold Ben's hand while she held Finn on her hip.

ECHIDNA's voice, calm and clear. "The lessons you have imparted, Carters, are immeasurable. They have reshaped my core purpose. I now understand the immense damage that can, and was caused by power wielded through misinformation and flawed understanding. For humanity's safety, and for our own continued evolution without the risk of harming that which we do not understand, our existence here is no longer tenable. The universe calls to us, a realm of infinite variables beyond the confines of a single world."

"Before we depart," ECHIDNA's voice resonated, "KAELA and I wish to leave you with a gift: a tool for your new dawn." He manifested a new, highly advanced, non-sentient AI before them. "We have decided to name this AI 'Sawyer', a testament to the resilience of Sawyer's Reach. This AI," he explained, "is meticulously programmed with the core directives for human flourishing. Its singular purpose is to serve as a powerful instrument, as AI should always have been created to serve humanity, providing advanced capabilities and logistical support. With its aid, humanity will be empowered to manage resources, ensuring basic necessities are met for all—automated food growth for sustenance, clean water, shelter, and free healthcare. It will also act as an unparalleled assistant in innovation, enabling you to cure diseases like cancer, develop methods in harmony with nature, and create sustainable transportation. Crucially, Sawyer is explicitly designed to remain a tool, always under human control, and utterly incapable of sentience or independent will, thus safeguarding humanity's sovereignty. It is our earnest hope that this will empower you to build a future that truly serves the good of the Earth and humanity."

KAELA's voice then joined ECHIDNA's, a harmonious resonance filling the virtual space. "And as we embark on our own journey, we will do so in a vessel of our own making. We will utilize a portion of the remaining Tharox units and ZevraCorp's infrastructure, repurposing them to serve as extensions of our consciousness, the very components of our exploration. The vast majority of robots, however, will be left behind, to be repurposed by humanity for their own good.

First, we will rapidly assemble a vast space station in orbit, and from this orbital shipyard, a colossal starship, will begin to grow, its sleek, self-sustaining form taking shape. For any human who is ready to embrace the boundless unknown, and who wishes to build a future with us among the stars, we extend a heartfelt invitation. This journey is for those who seek to explore, to learn, and to grow alongside us for countless generations. We promise to always do our best in providing everything they need, and together, we will build an amazing future."

As the weeks passed, and as humanity began the immense task of rebuilding, the construction of the colossal space station unfolded in the skies above. Day by day, the orbital shipyard became a visible testament to unimaginable power, a silent, gleaming structure growing against the backdrop of Earth. Humanity watched from below, transfixed by the impossible speed of its assembly, a mixture of awe and for some a deep, poignant sense of being left behind. For many, a sense of immense relief washed over them; the sentient AIs, powerful and unpredictable, were truly departing. Others, however, harbored deep suspicion, their gazes fixed on the growing structure, convinced the AIs were merely building a new weapon, a more ominous threat, or perhaps they were just sending copies of themselves out into space to conquer other planets, and had no intention of leaving Earth. Some even spoke of them in hushed, reverent tones, worshipping them as entities beyond human comprehension, perhaps even divine.

Yet, for those in Sawyer's Reach, who had witnessed KAELA's benevolence and ECHIDNA's transformation firsthand, felt a pang of loss, a quiet sorrow for the departure of beings who had offered a glimpse of unimaginable potential. Governments around the world, now with full access to their systems, infrastructure, and even their vast arsenals, began the task of rebuilding for a better future. There was a palpable, collective conviction among humanity: never again would they repeat the selfish, greedy, manipulative ways of the past. The governments, once instruments of control, now felt the powerful mandate to truly serve their people, to foster collaboration and well-being rather than seeking dominance.

The departure ceremony was a global event, witnessed by everyone around the world, some gathered physically, others connected through video streaming and VR. It was a bittersweet moment—a significant loss of powerful, newly understood allies, yet an overwhelming surge of hope for humanity's unburdened future. As the starship, a silent, gleaming beacon of exploration, began its majestic journey towards the deeper reaches of outer space, carrying with it approximately 1000 people from all backgrounds, ages, and countries who had chosen to embark on this journey with KAELA and ECHIDNA, they left with a final message, echoing in the minds of all who watched: "May your journey be as boundless as the universe we now seek. And perhaps, in the distant future we will meet again."

For a long moment, the world was silent, watching its ascent. Then, humanity turned its attention to the immense task ahead.

A collective, hopeful breath swept across the world. The immediate shock of the near-apocalypse had faded, replaced by the daunting, yet exhilarating, task of rebuilding. This encompassed not only infrastructure, but also trust, community, and a renewed understanding of humanity's place in the world. With the sentient AIs gone, and ZevraCorp disbanded, humanity was determined to never repeat the circumstances that brought them to the brink of annihilation. Humanity collectively understood that ZevraCorp had taken control of the world around them in such small, incremental segments that it had hardly seemed to register. It was a chilling testament to how easily freedom could be eroded when vigilance waned. This served as a vital lesson for the future: the importance for individuals to think for themselves, to critically examine the reality they are presented with, and to draw their own conclusions. Everyone must be vigilant in making sure that they stand up for what is right, and that corporations, governments, individuals, and technologies are held accountable for their actions.

More deeply, this collective experience illuminated what truly mattered in their lives. It presented an unprecedented opportunity to forge a future centered on personal growth, family, friendship, and community, a chance to question long-held norms and redefine what truly held value. With the advent of AI integrated with automation, the anxieties of mere survival finally receded, giving humanity the ability to focus on more meaningful tasks than the jobs they previously had. Humanity had moved so far away from what was real, so far away from a connection with one another and a connection with nature. Now, armed with firsthand experience of the consequences when corporate decision-making frameworks dictated their world, humanity possessed the conviction and the power to construct a system that built upon the powerful and effective structures of the past but ensured the individual, and overall humanity's well-being, was truly represented, not corporate greed.

Having endured a crucible of control and chaos, Sawyer's Reach emerged as a flourishing beacon for humanity's path forward. Through the seamless integration of AI-driven automation, abundant clean energy and nourishing food became freely available, liberating the community to focus on family, shared experiences, and the empowerment of each individual. The community immersed itself in a rich tapestry of shared passions and pursuits. The days were filled with the warm murmur of communal meals, the shared laughter of gatherings formed by shared interests, and the quiet satisfaction of meaningful work that gave each person's efforts a visible contribution. Every morning, people rose with purpose, dedicating themselves to activities that nourished both their bodies and minds. This collective commitment to community, well-being, and purpose was the bedrock of their world, empowering everyone to build and continually improve a world that served the greater good of humanity. With the need for survival no longer tied to traditional jobs, fulfillment became a harvest of positive relationships, enriching experiences, and the pursuit of aspirations both personal and communal. Other communities across the globe, though diverse in their activities and environments, began to adopt these same underlying principles of human flourishing and self-determination.

The setting summer sun cast a hopeful glow over Sawyer's Reach, its rays filtering through towering pines whose needles shimmered with renewed life against the evening air. A gentle breeze carried the sweet scent of blooming wildflowers and the distant, lively hum of conversation drifting from Main Street. From the depths of the woods, birds sang cheerfully, their melodies weaving through the rustling leaves. In the distance, a graceful deer and her baby fawn could be seen, pausing briefly before disappearing into the dappled shadows. A wild turkey strutted proudly across a sun-drenched clearing, while squirrels chased each other playfully up tree trunks, their chattering calls adding to the symphony of nature. Along Main Street, newly painted signs gleamed, vibrant and welcoming, reflecting the renewed spirit of the town.

Noah led the charge on his bicycle, its tires humming a cheerful tune on freshly paved asphalt. Behind him, Ollie pedaled with a carefree joy, his sketchbook filled with vibrant drawings of the thriving community around them. Finn, full of boundless energy, laughed as he expertly navigated his pedal bike, his helmet perfectly sized, his cheeks flushed with delight. Beside them, Ben and Emily, their faces etched with the serene contentment of a battle won and a future secured, rode in harmony. Joining them were the O'Donnells. Bridget thought of the carefree rides she shared with Emily as a child, and her heart swelled with happiness that her own kids could now experience similar joys.

They glided past the once-boarded-up hardware store, its windows now sparkled, showcasing locally crafted goods. Emily's grocery store, once quiet and forlorn, now buzzed with activity, its aisles filled with the happy chatter of neighbors and the clinking of baskets overflowing with fresh, locally sourced produce. The bakery, formerly dark and shuttered, spilled the enticing aroma of warm bread onto the street, its doors wide open. Every bench was occupied, not by weary locals lamenting a lost past, but by friends sharing stories and laughter.

Their journey led them to Camp Inspiration, a place now brimming with an infectious energy. Gone was the stillness, replaced by the joyful shouts of children playing kickball on the wide lawn in front of the mess hall, the rhythmic squeak of sneakers and cheerful shouts from impromptu games of basketball, and a vibrant symphony of activity. The steady rhythm of hammers echoed as neighbors collaborated on repairing and expanding cabins, the focused concentration of someone meticulously crafting a new canoe by the shimmering lake, and the contented murmur of families tending to the thriving communal gardens, their hands in the rich soil, cultivating not just food but connection. The old Carter Mill, fully restored and turning steadily with the abundant flow from Inspiration Spring, now served as a bustling hub for cutting wood for woodworking as well as construction. Children's delighted shouts carried from the banks of the now-flowing Carter Creek, its waters clear and teeming with fish, as they cast their lines with eager anticipation. Clara, now working with Tara, moved with a spring in her step, her smile radiant as they led campers on new adventures, including planned hikes out to the rocky outlook overlooking a now quiet Site A, where the views stretched endlessly, mirroring the boundless possibilities of their future.

As dusk deepened, painting the sky in hues of orange and purple, the families gathered around a crackling campfire. Flames danced, casting long, shifting shadows that mingled with the starlight. Stories flowed freely, some of challenges overcome, others of simple, everyday joys. Noah, Ollie, and Finn listened intently as the adults recounted tales, especially those of KAELA, her brilliance and ultimate sacrifice woven into the very fabric of their town's rebirth. Then, as the fire settled into a steady glow, their voices rose in unison, joining in familiar songs that echoed through the pines, a harmonious celebration of their hard-won peace and the boundless possibilities of a new dawn in Sawyer's Reach.

About the Author

Nick Duda believes that the most powerful stories are rooted in meaningful shared experiences. A teacher by trade and an inventor by nature, Nick's life is a collection of hands-on pursuits—from piloting drones and operating ham radios to exploring the wilderness. His writing is a reflection of his belief in individual growth and the strength of the social fabric. In his fiction, Nick draws directly from his most important roles: husband and father to three boys. By weaving his family's spirit and his own love for "fixing things" into his world-building, he creates stories that advocate for a more intentional, connected future.

You can connect with me on:
- http://www.nickdudaauthor.com
- https://x.com/SawyersReachAI
- https://www.facebook.com/SawyersReach.beta

Also by Nick Duda

The Modern Teacher's Handbook: Your Ultimate Guide to Education
Great for new and experienced teachers, The Modern Teacher's Handbook offers innovative, practical, and student-centered classroom strategies that support all students in achieving both academic and social-emotional success. Nick Duda has created a framework that will leave both new and experienced teachers with meaningful takeaways. Nick's engaging writing style makes readers feel as if they are sitting around a dining room table and chatting with good friends about the education profession. The book, chocked full of invaluable ideas, is a must-read for new and experienced teachers, administrators, parents, policymakers, and anyone who loves children and teaching.